THE KENNEDY-DEVONSHIRE CONNECTION

THE KENNEDY-DEVONSHIRE CONNECTION

Bernard Hackley

The Book Guild Ltd
Sussex, England

First published in Great Britain in 2002 by
The Book Guild Ltd,
25 High Street,
Lewes, East Sussex
BN7 2LU

Typesetting in Baskerville by
IML Typographers, Birkenhead, Merseyside

Printed in Great Britain by
Bookcraft (Bath) Ltd, Avon

A catalogue record for this book is
available from The British Library

ISBN 1 85776 617 2

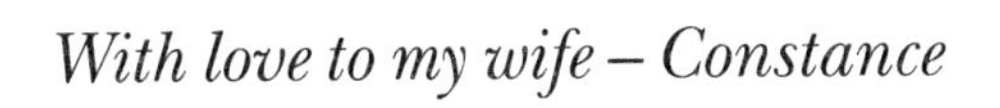

With love to my wife – Constance

FOREWORD

The main characters in this book were real persons. The book is based on the extraordinary and tragic relationship between two families, but it is a novel and employs the sort of licence that is customary in a work of fiction. I have done my best to ensure that there are no errors of chronological or historical fact, but if there are then they are mine alone, probably to retain the result of these recordings that are done for dramatic purposes.

B E Hackley

1

Hurrying down the steps of the Pentagon, Cordell Hull, the Secretary of State, jumped into his waiting car. His bodyguard, who followed him wherever he went, made his customary look around and stepped into the seat beside the driver.

It was a miserable, cold and wet afternoon in November 1937, but he had more to worry about than the weather. He had had a most unsatisfactory day and now had to report back to the President. It had been an impossible task from the start; there had not been the slightest chance that any members of the Administration would agree that Joe be given a senior appointment amongst them. It had been bad enough trying to persuade them, putting forward all the points he could think of in his favour, when he himself was all against Joe being given a senior job in the government, but the President was stuck with him, and he saw no alternative.

"George, make it as fast as you can, I am already late for my appointment with the President."

"Yes, Sir." His driver of long standing wove his way as fast as he could up Pennsylvania Avenue, past the headquarters of the FBI, ruled by J. Edgar Hoover. In a few minutes, in spite of the traffic, George drove into the very private rear entrance of the White House.

His car, having been cleared at the security checkpoint, drew up at the entrance of the President's private offices. Hull hurried inside, handed over his coat and hat and made his way towards the very centre of power – the Oval Office. Although well known, he flashed his identity card at the military guard standing at the entrance to the office of the President's Private Secretary, from which a door led to the door of the inner sanctum. "Hello, Mary," he said.

Mary Brand had been FDR's secretary from way back. She was privy to all the intrigues, scandals, secrets and all the wheeling and dealing that went on behind the scenes in the running of the government. She knew all about the problem that had brought about the impasse.

"You look your bright and cheerful self today," said Hull. Mary smiled – they were old friends. She would have liked to have been in the office when the President gave him the news. She pressed the intercom button connected with the President's office and announced that he had arrived.

"He's been waiting for you," she said. "Go right in."

He entered the office of the President. Franklin D. Roosevelt was seated behind his massive desk. He was an impressive figure. His crippled legs, which made walking so difficult and arduous, were hidden from view.

"Come in, Cordell, good to see you." His friendly smile, open countenance, mop of iron-grey wavy hair and sparkling eyes behind his rimless glasses gave him the appearance of being one of the most friendly and easy-going persons to get along with – they belied the brilliant, calculating brain that had carried him to his present position.

FDR was in his second term. He had been disappointed in the smallness of his majority. Fortunately, the country had come out of the great depression of the early thirties, and he had been helped by the huge government spending programme. He had engineered many of the large capital building projects and had authorised, in conjunction with the Chiefs of Staff of the US Armed Forces, a great increase in the defence capability of the country. Intelligence had reported that the Japanese were building a fleet of battleships and aircraft carriers. This information, together with the news that the Germans had also embarked on a great naval expansion programme building battleships and a large number of submarines, was of great concern. Of course, the British Navy should be able to contain any threat from any quarter. America, whilst not expecting to be involved in any conflict that did not affect their own interests, must remain the most powerful of all nations, and plans had been put in hand to expand all branches of the services and to bring them up to date.

"I'm sorry that I'm a little late, Mr President," said Hull. "It's taken me longer for me to get around and to see everyone to argue the case. We agreed that they should all have the opportunity to express their views."

"That's OK," said FDR. He glanced at the typed sheet of appointments in front of him, every hour accounted for. "We have twenty minutes. You don't look very cheerful – how did you get on?"

"As soon as I put forward the proposition that you bring Joe into the Administration, every one of them, without exception, objected strongly – very strongly. They do not want him at any price. I told them that you cannot possibly afford to drop him – they all know that."

"You're quite right," said FDR. "I cannot possibly dump him. Joe Kennedy has supported me and the Party from years back. He has poured vast amounts of money into our funds. During the last elections he has been all round the country drumming up votes for me. He and his father-in-law, John Fitzgerald, have between them virtually tied up the Irish-American vote, not only in Massachusetts but throughout the country. I could not possibly lose that support under any circumstances."

"So what can you do?" said Hull. "If that is the case, there seems to be no alternative, despite what we all think, but to join the team – that is what he wants, and what he thinks he is entitled to. I see no alternative. Of course, you will have members of the government wanting to see you to complain. You know what happened when you appointed him to chair the Committee to make the Stock Exchange subject to strict rules and regulations. You had everyone, and all the Press, objecting strongly because we all knew the way Joe played the market and had made a terrific fortune. Still, I must admit he made a damn good job of putting the Exchange in order."

"I know, I know," said FDR. "But whatever happens, I cannot risk dumping him, and for him to go over the other side. You know the support he has. Look at the effect it would have on the Party vote – our majority is small enough as it is."

"So if that is the case," said Hull, "there is no alternative, despite what I have reported, but to bring him into the government. Do you think he wants my job?" They both laughed.

"No, I think he wants mine," replied FDR. "I waited until I heard your report and have decided that I will not bring him into the government. You've heard the British say 'If you can't kick them down, kick them upstairs' – that's what I am going to do with Joe."

"I don't get it."

"I've been in touch with George in London. He's done a

very good job there, but both he and his wife are getting on. They have really enjoyed being there, but they feel that they would like to come back home and settle down. So I have decided to let them come back and to make Joe Kennedy the US Ambassador in London. What do you think?"

Cordell Hull was flabbergasted. "Good God!" he said. "That's one I would never have thought up – but will Joe buy it? As soon as you suggest it he'll know that he's been sidetracked. You know his political ambitions – this will take him out of the running completely. I think he'll be furious – what if he refuses?"

"Of course I have thought of that, but I do not see how he can refuse. After all, it is the most prestigious appointment in the diplomatic set-up. If he does not accept, where does that leave him? He would be out on a limb. He is being offered one of the most important jobs representing us in the world. If he turns it down, he cannot expect to be offered anything else. The appointment is always given by the President to someone who has supported the Party financially and is rich enough to see the job through. Although it's very well paid, you have to have a substantial private income to handle the job well – so who better than Joe?"

"Well, I hope that you can sell the idea."

"I don't see why not," said FDR. "I know that he will be furious at being left out of the government, but when he has thought it through it may appeal to his ego. But I will tell you something – Rose will be over the moon. The Kennedy clan have three things close to their hearts: money, power and family prestige, and despite all their money they are not in with the top twenty here – the Vanderbilts, the Rockefellers and their clique. This appointment will give Rose the social life that she could never have dreamed of. She will love meeting the King and Queen and mixing with all the upper crust."

"I think that it's a brilliant solution. It will certainly get Joe out of our hair. I hope that you can bring it off," said Hull. "But there is one major problem: Joe is always boasting of his bog-Irish background. He's a damn sight more pro-Irish than British. I don't feel that the British will think much of the idea at all. Normally we tell them, out of courtesy, who we have in mind for the job, and they usually agree, but this time it's different. Have you made any contact with them about appointing Joe? The last thing they will want is a pro-Irish American Ambassador in London. I think that they will take a very poor view of the appointment."

"You're quite right," replied FDR, "so I haven't consulted them. In this case they will have to accept the position. I have to get rid of Joe. If he accepts, as I think he will have to, then we will just publish the appointment formally and advise the British. As you say, Chamberlain and his Cabinet will not think much of it. I'll have to placate them. They're having enough headaches without anyone stirring up the Irish menace. We shall have to keep a close watch on Joe."

"Well, Mr President," said Hull, "I wish you luck with him – I don't envy you."

FDR's eyes sparkled. "When you aspire to become the President of the United States, this is the sort of problem you have to expect to deal with. I'll let you know as soon as I've seen Joe."

"I certainly hope that you can fix it," said Hull. He stood up to take his leave.

"Good day, Cordell. Thanks for your efforts."

As Hull left the office, FDR pressed the intercom button on his desk. "Mary, please get in touch with Senator Kennedy and ask him to come and see me tomorrow."

FDR sat back in his chair and mused. Joe had been one of his most generous and loyal supporters – he owed him a lot. Knowing Joe's political ambitions, he did not like what he had to do.

* * *

Senator Joe Kennedy, sitting in the family apartment no great distance from the White House, finished his breakfast and his third cup of coffee. He reached for the pile of newspapers on the table in front of him and glanced at the headlines. Normally at this time he would be on his way to the Senate. He was waiting for a phone call.

The apartment was home base for him when he was in Washington. Rose and the family only came down from Boston when there was some official or social function they had to attend. At the present time he was the only occupant of the apartment. This suited him well. The daily maid arrived each morning, prepared his breakfast and left about midday. Joe rarely required an evening meal, usually dining at his club. Louise, the maid, had to be most careful that she cleaned away any evidence of those occasions when he spent the evening enjoying the company of a member of the opposite sex.

He was feeling exasperated: why had they not been in touch with him? It was common knowledge that FDR was, twelve months after the Presidential election of '36, rearranging the senior posts of his Administration. He was impatient to know which of the six top jobs he would be offered. He well knew that his face did not fit with the rest of them. What the hell – FDR was the one who decided, and FDR owed him. All the years he had supported him – all the money he had poured into the party – and most of all, the Irish votes, which he virtually controlled. FDR could not afford to let him down: he had too much to lose. He did not mind which of the top jobs he was offered. Once in, he knew it would be a stepping stone to the top.

The phone rang and a familiar voice came on the line. "Hello, Senator, this is Mary. I tried to get you last evening without success. The President wishes you to come and see him at three o'clock this afternoon – is that OK?"

"Thank you, Mary, I'll be there. Tell the President that I'll be there. I look forward to seeing him." He was flying back to Boston the following day; the whole family would be there – he would be able to tell them the great news.

* * *

He was ushered into the inner sanctum.

"Hello, Joe. My, but it is good to see you." FDR exuded his usual charm. "How are you? You look fine. Tell me Joe, how are the family? Has Rose been off on any of her long trips abroad lately? They tell me that Joe Junior is already getting himself well known in the Party. Never too young to start. He should go far – you must be proud of him. And what about young Jack – how is he keeping?"

"I'm pleased to say that his health is much better. I'm sure he'll be OK."

"You sure have a sizeable family to look after: nine is a pretty good score. And what about young Kathleen – has she finished school? She sure is a sweetie."

"Yes, she's just finished at the High School Convent. She's already looking very grown-up," said Joe. Why the hell did he not get on with it?

"Well, Joe, I did not ask you to come just to talk about

old times," said FDR. "As you know, I am having to make some changes in the Administration."

Joe sat back – this was what he had been waiting for: this was it.

"We are very concerned at what is happening in Europe. We have to more than ever before be closely in touch with events to watch our interests so as to decide what line we are to take. I'm not at all happy with this fellow Hitler – I would not trust him at all. At the same time, I do not intend to get this country involved in a European war. I had hoped to bring you into the Administration, but the situation has changed. As you know, George in London is getting on: he feels that he would like to come back home and settle down, so I must have someone in London to be on top of the situation – use his position to be able to keep us informed of every move. Someone who has the ability, contacts and energy to do that for us. In fact there is nobody better suited to look after the interests of this country at this time than yourself, Joe. I want you to accept the most important of all our diplomatic appointments abroad – to be the US Ambassador to Britain in London."

Kennedy felt the anger rising within him. The bastards – they had sidelined him. FDR had fixed it. After all the money, all the work and all the support and all the votes he had got for the Party, they had ditched him. All his efforts to get political power had come to nothing. He had only one card to play, and he made his pitch.

"Well, to say the least, I'm overwhelmed," said Joe. "I am quite honoured to be offered this very important post, but I'm afraid there is one obstacle that makes it quite impossible for me to accept. As you know, my background is Irish, and I have great affection for the Irish and for their aspirations for a united Ireland. I am sure that the

British Government would not wish to have a US Ambassador who is pro a united Ireland. In view of the delicate situation in Europe, I think that it would be advisable if you appoint someone else. In saying this, I would not wish you to think that I wouldn't be happy to be considered for an appointment in the Administration – you know my services to you and the Party over all these years."

"That's just the point, Joe," replied FDR. "By going to London with your known background, you will be able to take a neutral stance with the British. Britain feels that there is an unofficial bond between us and them, but because of the Hitler menace we must not be in a position where we are tied to anyone – the country would not stand for it. In any event, Joe, the changes that I'm making are not important enough for anyone of your ability – so there it is. I'm sure that your feelings for the Irish would in no way affect what would be best for us when dealing with the British."

Kennedy knew that he was cornered – they wanted him out of the way. He kept his temper with the greatest difficulty – there would be no job worth having here. "Well, Mr President," he said, "I've given you my views. I feel that I could have served the country better here in Washington, but if you feel that it is in the interest of the country that I go to London, then of course I have no alternative but to accept."

"I'm delighted that you appreciate the position, Joe. I'll contact Chamberlain and have the appointment published immediately. I'm sure that it will be a wonderful experience for both Rose and yourself, and all the family – give them by best wishes."

"Goodbye, Mr President: give my best wishes to Eleanor."

"I will, I will," said FDR.

Joe felt that he had to get that one in: it was common knowledge that the only time FDR saw his wife was at official functions. Their marriage had been a façade for years – he found matrimonial comforts elsewhere.

Joe smiled bleakly to Mary on his way out. He felt dazed. The job in London would give him entrée to a world where he would have considerable influence and power, but his pride had been hurt and his political aspirations ruined.

Kennedy returned to his apartment and, over a large Scotch, brooded over the future. So be it. He felt vindictive: if they thought that they had squeezed the Kennedys out of the political arena, they had another think coming. Joe Kennedy Junior was young but he had good looks, personality, and flair and was already very popular with the top brass of the Party. Money was what counted in the political rat race. Well, he had the money: he would build up his son Joe, provide all the funds necessary. It would take years – he would have to be patient – but one day a Kennedy would be the President of the most powerful country in the world: the USA.

FDR rang for his secretary to come in. "Mary, first of all circularise everyone about Joe's appointment – that will sure create a stir. Then write Chamberlain: the usual, hope he is well, then say that our present Ambassador is retiring and that we have appointed Mr Joseph Kennedy to replace him. Say that I am sure that he will prove to be an excellent choice and will serve us both very well. I'll sign it personally. I know that he won't like it, but he will have to put up with it."

2

Edward Cavendish, Lord Hartington, heir to the ninth Duke of Devonshire, left the offices of the Jockey Club in the West End of London and hailed a taxi to take him to his Club. He was the president of the Jockey Club – an organisation unique in the annals of British sport. It had been formed 150 years previously and, from the beginning, had controlled all facets of horse racing in Britain.

From the day it was formed, the Presidency had always been held by a member or a nominee of the Devonshire family, usually the Duke or his heir. On archaic lines, the members of the governing body were always members of the establishment, if a member died or could no longer serve, the other members chose who would be the replacement. They supervised all matters relating to the sport venues, trainers, jockeys – imposed fines, even expulsions: a very strange way to run the horse-racing industry, but with a large staff it worked.

Seated in the lounge of his Club, Lord Hartington picked up *The Times*; but he could not concentrate on the news: Before leaving his London home he had received a phone call from his mother. The news was not unexpected – his father had been ill for some time and was dying. He had known since childhood that one day he would become the next Duke of Devonshire. The Devonshires had, throughout the centuries, been one of the most important and richest families in the country. As well as their great mansion, Chatsworth House, they owned several large properties throughout the land – over a quarter of a million acres in Britain, as well as a medieval castle, Lismore, in Ireland, with its own 7,000 acres.

Whilst on a visit to Lismore, his father had suffered a stroke. He had recovered, but his whole personality had changed. He became almost impossible to live with, bad-tempered and irritable. When he inherited the title he was sorry that he was unable to continue with his political ambitions. During the war, and immediately after, he served as Governor General of Canada, where he was very popular. After the war he settled down to handle his vast estates in much the same way that they had managed throughout the centuries. As he was now quite incapable of handling his affairs, his wife took over control of all the estates. She was most efficient, but quite a dragon. Shortly after his stroke, she organised the formation of a private company, which held all the assets in trust for Lord Hartington, thereby saving millions in Death Duties that would have had to have been paid. So, at the age of 45, he would become the 10th Duke of Devonshire, and his eldest son, William, would assume his title of Lord Hartington.

Like his father, he had always had great political ambitions – always the staunchest Conservative, a large financial supporter of the Party, traditionally controlling the seat of West Derbyshire. He might have got a seat in the Cabinet: now he would have to be satisfied with a seat in the Lords.

"I say, Hartington," his thoughts were interrupted by the Club bore, Charlie Heston, sitting opposite him. "What do you think of the Americans appointing that chap Joe Kennedy as Ambassador here? I think it's a bloody disgrace. By all accounts, he's pro-Irish and no lover of Britain."

"I don't know him – I've never met him," replied Hartington. Little did he realise how this appointment would affect the lives of this family, the Devonshires, and the lives of the Kennedys in the years to come: how they would be so closely and tragically connected.

3

Neville Chamberlain, Prime Minister of Britain, sitting at his desk at 10 Downing Street, waved the letter he had received from FDR at his Foreign Secretary, Lord Halifax, sitting opposite him. "Frankly, Halifax, I am most annoyed that Roosevelt should have made this appointment without consulting me first."

He looked tired: he had had a terrible year – that man Hitler had made his life impossible. Months earlier, Hitler had marched into the Sudetenland and had threatened Czechoslovakia, parading all his military might. It seemed that, despite all the pleas from Chamberlain, he would invade. Then, at the last moment, he invited Chamberlain to visit him at his country retreat, the Eagle's Nest. Swallowing his pride he went, and Hitler assured him that he had no further military ambitions in Europe. They signed a peace pact.

Chamberlain had returned to London in triumph – peace in our time – there will be no war. The world sighed with relief.

As if he had not had enough to worry about abroad, at home in Britain there was a new threat – Fascism. An erstwhile Conservative MP, Sir Oswald Mosley, had formed the British Fascist Party on the same lines as Hitler's Nazi Party. The same techniques were being used – gangs of thugs wearing their blackshirt uniforms, financed by Mosley – well organised to make provocative marches, largely against the Jews, these marches taking place in the East End of London, with its predominately Jewish population. There were many fights and clashes with the police. The movement was soundly condemned in the media and by the public. There was great demand that they should be disbanded, but in a democracy in peacetime that was easier said than done.

"Tell me," said Chamberlain, "what do we know about Kennedy?"

"It's well known that he's very rich," replied Halifax. "My researchers have been digging into his background. Apparently, he managed to stay out of the war by getting a job with Bethlehem Steel and then got a contract to feed the American Forces – this seems to have been the founding of his fortune. His father owned liquor stores in Boston, which were affected by Prohibition, but apparently he had contacts during that time. His real wealth came from his wheeler-dealing on Wall Street. He moved into the motion-picture industry and made a lot of money. Despite being a staunch Roman Catholic, he is said to be quite a lad with the ladies. He's reported to have had an affair with Gloria Swanson which lasted for years. He has a very large family.

He and Roosevelt have been very close, politically, for years: he's poured money into the funds of the Democratic Party. He's disliked by all the senior members of the Party – they know that he wants a top job. Roosevelt cannot upset them, so he has dumped him on us. We know that he is pro-Irish, and the last thing we want at the present time is to have a pro-Irish American Ambassador, but what can we do? They can appoint whom they wish. If the worst came to the worst and we were faced with a war, we could not quarrel with the USA: we would need their moral and material support."

Chamberlain sighed. He had lost the support of several of his senior colleagues over his policy of appeasement, none more so than Anthony Eden, his previous Foreign Secretary. To make matters worse, Eden had joined forces with Winston Churchill who, although he was not in the government, was raising hell, accusing him of giving way to Hitler.

He dreaded the very thought of war – he remembered the last war. Despite their recent pact, could he trust Hitler to keep his word? He was already receiving news that he was making military moves. What could he do? Britain was quite unprepared to fight a major war – the equipment of the armed forces was completely out of date. Thank heaven that the British Navy was still the most powerful in the world. At least his agreement with Hitler had allowed him to play for time. He had put in hand a vast programme of rearmament. Orders had been placed with British industry to manufacture as soon as possible every type of modern weapons of war. In the air, Britain had produced a fighter plane, the Spitfire, which by all accounts would be able to compete with any plane that the Germans had.

4

No sooner had the DC3 flight from Washington touched down at Boston Airport than Joe Kennedy hurried down the steps and climbed into his car, which was waiting for him on the tarmac. He hardly acknowledged his driver's greeting – he was seething with anger. He did not relish telling the family that he had failed to get a major post in the administration. "Home as soon as you can." His driver kept quiet – he knew Kennedy's moods.

The car drew up at the entrance of the large mansion, which stood in its spacious grounds. He handed his hat and coat to the maid at the door and entered the lounge, where the family was waiting for him. Rose, with her usual show of outward affection, kissed him and he, as was the custom, kissed all the family in turn.

"Let's have it, Pa, what did you get?" Joe Junior had just returned from a trip to Germany that his father had arranged, to meet, as he put it, people that mattered.

"If you mean what top job in the government did I get – well I didn't." The room went silent; they sensed the mood he was in. When he was like that, the best thing to do was to keep quiet. "No – FDR has sidetracked me. He didn't give me an appointment – after all I've done for him."

"But he can't, Joe – he can't drop you like that after all these years," cried Rose.

"What I mean is that he hasn't given me the sort of job in government that I'm entitled to; he's given me no alternative but to accept the most important appointment in the Diplomatic Corps – the US Ambassador to Britain in London."

They were all flabbergasted at the news. Rose was the first to recover. "Oh, Joe, I'm so sorry that you didn't get what you wanted, but I can see that you couldn't refuse such a wonderful appointment."

"Of course it is a wonderful appointment, but it isn't what I wanted. I don't know how I shall get on with that lot over there."

Rose was secretly elated. She saw the whole world opening before her – mixing with all the members of the Court, even the King and Queen – all the top people.

Her mind flashed back to her teens. Her father, the flamboyant John Fitzgerald, Mayor of Boston, held the city in the palm of his hand. Her mother was a shrinking violet who did not like the social functions, the balls, the parties that went with the office, so Rose, in her teens, had been his official companion: an acting mayoress. She travelled around with him everywhere. She loved it all – the centre of attraction. The family were staunch Roman Catholics and very much leaders of the pro-Irish community in the district. Rose, at an early age, had no illusions: her father used the very convenient social round to give himself the opportunities to enjoy the favours of the opposite sex. Perhaps this background was why Rose, after her marriage to Joe, chose to ignore his shortcomings in that direction.

As soon as Rose had left school, she and Joe were always in each other's company. John Fitzgerald and Joe's father were the leaders of the Democrat Party throughout the district. It seemed natural that Joe and Rose should get married. They had raised a large family and Rose, because of Joe being away so much, handed the children over to a series of nannies to enable her to enjoy travelling around herself.

For Kathleen, recently released from the confines of a Roman Catholic convent at 18, the news that they were going to Britain and all that was involved was wonderful – a great adventure. Attractive, vivacious and charming, she was very mature for her age. She was thrilled at the prospect.

Her sister Rosemary smiled; they did not know whether she understood what it was all about. Joe and Rose tried to keep mentally retarded Rosemary's activities within the orbit of the family; it was most difficult.

* * *

Joe Kennedy took up his appointment as the US Ambassador to Britain in March 1938. He managed to find a large house very near the embassy. Rose and the family followed a few weeks later. He duly presented his credentials to the King, wearing a long-tailed morning suit and carrying a top hat – the boys pulled his leg unmercifully on what they called his monkey suit. He was well received by the King, who stressed the importance of the US and Britain working in unison in order to contain the Hitler threat. Joe was most diplomatic in agreeing about Britain and the States' great friendship, but was very careful not to say anything which might be construed as a commitment. In his heart, he knew that he would do everything he could to see that the States would not be involved in any conflict in Europe.

Shortly after, they were invited by the King and Queen to stay as their guests at Windsor Castle. They were overwhelmed by the grandeur of the castle – the great reception and state rooms, the library with its ancient and priceless volumes, the splendour of St George's Chapel, where the spectacle of the assembly of the Knights of the Garter is held annually. They enjoyed their tour of the battlements, from where they could look across the river Thames to see the village of Eton and the college beyond.

Expressing interest in the school, they were escorted over the bridge between Windsor and Eton. They stopped to look at the numerous antique shops and the small, old-fashioned, traditional tea shops in the village. The Headmaster took them on a tour of the College and gave them details of all the rituals which were still carried out exactly as they had been for hundreds of years. They were inwardly amused at the pupils' clothes – the black morning dress of the seniors and the short jackets of the juniors. It was very different to the garb worn in high schools in the States.

From the front of the castle they could see the road – the Long Walk, where the royal family drove in open carriages down to Ascot racecourse at the end of the Walk on the occasion of the Royal Ascot race meetings: a very royal procession, to be acclaimed by the race goers as they paraded in front of the stands en route to the Royal Box. They saw the daily spectacle of the Changing of the Guard. The regiment on duty, stationed in barracks in the town, provided the guard which, behind their band, marched to the castle – a grand sight for visitors from all over the world.

It was a grand time for the whole family. They were meeting and being entertained by the whole of British society. One of their most important contacts was the Astor family – a contact which was of considerable help to Joe when he was arguing his case for negotiating with Hitler.

Whereas the Irish Kennedys had emigrated and made their fortune in America, the Astors' story was strange in the extreme. Jacob Astor, the founder of the dynasty, made a vast fortune in the fur trade and prospecting. An immigrant from Central Europe, he pioneered the trade right across America, from New York to the west coast. He set up trading posts and bought furs from Indians and prospectors, eventually establishing his base in San Francisco. He successfully fought off the monopoly of the Canadian Hudson Bay Company, and from San Francisco he opened up trade with China.

His son, William Waldorf Astor, who inherited his vast fortune and all his property, which included quite a large piece of Manhattan, quarrelled with the US Treasury about the amount of tax which had to be paid on the estate. He had travelled to Britain, mixed with the aristocracy, liked what he saw and decided to be part of the scene. He realised most of his assets in America and bought two large estates in Britain: Hever Castle in Kent, the original home of Anne Boleyn, and a very elegant mansion, Cliveden, situated in the village of Taplow, near the Thameside town of Maidenhead. The house overlooked the Thames Valley and the spacious grounds ran down to the river. As a result of his wealth and his political activities he achieved his ambition – he became the first Viscount Astor. On his death he divided his estates between his two sons, Waldorf and Jacob. Waldorf took over Cliveden and Jacob took Hever Castle.

Before he inherited the title, Waldorf had entered British politics and succeeded in becoming the Conservative MP for Plymouth. He had married an

American girl, Nancy Shaw, a lady of very strong views and firm convictions, so when Waldorf succeeded to the title Nancy entered the fray. She got herself nominated by the Plymouth Conservative Party as their candidate for her husband's vacant seat, which she fought and won. She was the first woman MP in the British parliament – an American.

She soon made her presence felt in the House. Being the first lady MP and a very strong Conservative did not prevent her challenging the government on many issues. She was soon at loggerheads with Churchill – she was not his favourite MP.

Her husband, the second Viscount, had meanwhile procured the important newspaper, *The Observer*. His brother went one better and purchased the greatest of British newspapers, *The Times*. He eventually became Baron Astor of Hever.

In pursuit of her political ambitions, Lady Astor had gathered around her a clique of quite important personages known as the Cliveden Set. Their politics were extremely right-wing. They initially admired Hitler: the way he had transformed Germany – the efficiency of the nation. They were extremely anti-Communist. They felt that in no circumstances should Britain be involved in a European war: they were great supporters of Chamberlain's appeasement policy. On being challenged over Hitler's treatment of the Jews, they held that the reports had been greatly exaggerated. Their opinions caused quite a lot of concern in Westminster. However, *The Times* and *The Observer* took a more balanced view.

The views held by the Set were exactly the views that Joe wanted to hear. The family were invited to stay at Cliveden.

The visit was a great success. Joe liked holding forth to a receptive audience. In particular, Lady Astor took a great liking to Kathleen – a very useful contact for her.

Work at the embassy was going smoothly. Joe was beginning to enjoy his power and prestige. The chip on his shoulder was no longer so irksome. He still resented his treatment by FDR, but he was realising that, in the present international turmoil, he was in a position to exert pressure.

Joe Junior and Jack were sent on their separate ways for a further sightseeing tour of Europe. On his return, Joe was taken on as an Assistant Secretary at the American Embassy, his father making sure that he was kept in the picture. Jack's health was again causing concern. On his return he had to rest. He spent his time producing a book in which he was highly critical of the way the countries on the Continent were governed. He went out of his way to praise the way that Germany, under Hitler, had been regenerated – made proud of itself. It was well organised, its industrial capacity expanded. To some extent, he gave the same sort of credit to the Italian Fascist dictator, Mussolini. He compared them favourably with what he saw as the flabby democracies of Britain, France and other European countries, his views being jaundiced by the threat of international Communism.

His father paid for the publication of the book. It had a terrible Press, both in Britain and America. In America, his admiration of the German method of government was greatly resented by the Jewish community.

Joe Kennedy was livid – seated at the desk in his elegant office in the embassy, he stared at the letter he had received from the States. He picked up the phone. "Get my wife for me immediately," he declared. "If she is not in leave a message that she is to phone me immediately." Fortunately Rose was in.

"Do you know whether Joe and Jack are in town and where they are?" Joe asked.

"I believe they are, but I do not know their plans," she replied.

"Well, get in touch with them – I don't give a damn what their plans are – they must meet me at home this evening at six-thirty. I shall be coming directly from the embassy – they are to be there."

"I'll see if I can trace them," said Rose, "but of course they may not be able to get away."

"Get away! Tell them from me I insist that they be there – no excuses – they are to be there." Rose replaced the receiver. It was going to be one of those nights.

Joe Junior and Jack were waiting for him in the small room they used as an office when he stormed in.

Seating himself at the desk, he took from his pocket the letter he had received from the States. He glared at them.

"This is from Ben Rubenstein in New York, I know him quite well. He is not exactly a friend – more of a business acquaintance. He is the head of one of the largest financial houses in the States, and he has a lot of pull with the banks and with Washington. He is also a leading member of the Jewish Orthodox Church. I'll read out what he says. 'Like my friends, I am quite disgusted and appalled at the views expressed by your son John F. Kennedy following his recent tour of Europe. He seems to think that all the governments there are either inefficient, decadent or both – that is except Germany. Your son seems to applaud the way in which Hitler and his gang are ruling their country – the dictatorial and regimental way in which everyone is forced to live, the hate which is being expended against everyone who the Nazis say is not of German origin, the manner in which the Jews in Germany are now being treated. This hatred being manifested in beatings, burning of shops, hounding them out of business, stealing their property, subjecting them to every kind of humiliation. Your son appears to admire this evil monster Hitler who is bringing Europe to the brink of war. Are these your views too, Joe Kennedy? If so then the people of America should be made aware of them.' Signed Ben Rubenstein."

Joe turned to Jack and snarled, "Why the hell did you write that damn book?"

Jack replied, "Well, Pa, you agreed and said it would give me public image, that it was a good idea. You agreed to pay for the cost of production. I gave you a copy of the draft before it was published."

"I know I agreed but I was far too busy other than to give it a quick glance." He turned to Joe Junior. "If you saw the script why did you not warn me?" He knew it was no use arguing with his father – he would always blame someone else if things went wrong.

He replied, "Jack was laid up when he wrote the book. I was elsewhere. I should have seen the draft but I didn't. I wish to goodness that I had – I would certainly have tackled Jack on some of the views he expressed. When I visited Germany I saw the Nazis for what they were. I agree with Rubenstein; if that madman Hitler is not stopped he will try to rule Europe. Sorry, Jack, I feel I have let you down."

"All right, all right," said Joe, "this is what we will do. You, Jack, will write personally to Rubenstein. Tell him that you are most concerned at what he has written, that you now realise that you were hoodwinked by the Nazis and you are quite devastated to learn about the way the Jews were being treated in Germany, that you – say that you have instructed the publishers to destroy all the books in stock and call back from their customers any they have on show so that they can be destroyed. Give him your abject apologies for this unfortunate happening. I will write to him, also, and tell him that I had not seen the script before it was published. I will apologise for not having done so; I would certainly not have allowed the book to be printed. The last thing I wish to do is to upset the feelings of my many Jewish friends, and I trust that he will pass on my apologies on suitable occasions. God, what a mess. Jack, get on with it."

Later that evening Joe Junior sought out his mother. "I suppose you have heard about the row," he said.

"Oh yes," said Rose, "he always holds forth to me stating his side of any argument."

"I feel that I have let Jack down, but as you know the old man is always pushing me into the foreground and because of ill health Jack seems left out. Jack and I are the best of friends and I thought that this was a chance for him to get some kudos. Let's hope that the whole incident will blow over."

5

The Irish Government invited Joe to Dublin – it was to be one of the greatest events of his life. Accompanied by Joe Junior, he was given a terrific reception. The Government, in recognition of his services to the Irish people in America and of his support to the people of Ireland in their struggle to attain a United Ireland which would include Ulster, granted Joe an honorary degree at Dublin University. In his speech he left no doubt that he supported all their causes.

"This is a great day for me," he said, "I am so proud to have been given this great honour, just as I am proud that my forebears came from this beautiful land." (Cheers) "Just as I am proud of the way you struggle against the power of Britain to integrate Northern Ireland." (Loud cheers) "I am pleased to represent the thousands and thousands of Irish American citizens who look back on your land as their mother country.

"I am, and I am sure you are, very concerned at the problems facing the countries of Europe at this present time. The military strength and power of Germany is causing concern in Britain and France. They are making demands which are unlikely to be met. Hitler has agreed to meetings to discuss these problems but Britain and France show no signs of meeting these demands and seem to be getting to a point of war. In this event I say to you that despite the pressure that will be put on you, you will never allow yourselves to be drawn into such a conflict. What of America? I can say with confidence that there is a great feeling throughout the country not to be drawn into such a conflict. We are at peace – we all want peace – and I shall use all my efforts whenever and wherever I am to maintain peace.

"And so may I once again thank you for the great honour you have done to me today." Joe sat down to thunderous applause.

In London the speech was highly criticised in the Press. The British Government were not at all pleased – it was clear that their fears that Joe Kennedy was not a suitable Ambassador representing the United States were justified. Washington did not like the speech: they played it down.

The morning after the speech, in a private room at the American Embassy where they had stayed overnight prior to their return to London, Joe and Joe Junior waited for their visitors. Joe was in the best of moods: the reception he had received the day before had boosted his ego. Joe felt that in London, despite all the outward show of goodwill which he and his family had been shown, underneath it all he was, to say the least, not very well liked or, for that matter, trusted.

Here in Ireland, he was back to the family roots – here they really appreciated him. "Mr Kennedy, may we say on behalf of all our members what a great honour and privilege it is to meet you."

His visitors had been welcomed and were seated comfortably with a generous glass of Irish whiskey in their hands. Their visit had been kept quiet. They were the President and Financial Secretary of the Irish Northern

Aid Committee. Their activities were not made public, but their aims were blazoned all over the world. Their object was to further the cause of reunification of all Ireland.

Their job was to raise money and to distribute this to support this aim. The main source of this income came from the Irish communities in America, and who had done more to support their cause than the Kennedys? not only by propaganda – look at Joe's speech yesterday – but by the very generous sums of cash that had been donated over the years. The Committee secured large sums of money, but how it was distributed was never disclosed. They stated that it was all spent in propaganda in support of their cause. They strongly denied that the money was used for the purchase of arms and ammunition for the use of the terrorists, the Irish Republican Army – the IRA.

The 'hail fellow well met' meeting ended in Joe promising his continued support and receiving the grateful thanks of his visitors.

Turning to his son after they had gone, Joe said, "I think those guys are doing a damn good job. I think our money is being well spent."

"Watch it, Pa," said Joe Junior.

"What do you mean, watch it?" replied Joe.

"You are the US Ambassador to Britain – you must be impartial between all sides. If you continue to shout the odds on the question of the unification of Ireland the British are not going to like it at all. Washington will not think much of it either."

"Bah! You're exaggerating," said Joe, "I know what I'm doing."

Joe Junior sighed. No one told his father what to do.

6

Andrew, the second son of the Duke of Devonshire, turned to his elder brother. They were sitting in the bar of the Army and Navy Club in the West End of London. They were both in the British Army Reserve – very senior officers attached to the Coldstream Guards. In the event of war breaking out, they would be amongst the first to be called up.

"Bill, quite honestly I cannot say that I am sorry that Grandfather has died: he's been a pain in the neck to both of us since we were kids. In fact he virtually ruddy well ignored us."

"I quite agree," replied the new Lord Hartington. "When Grandma has moved out of Chatsworth into Hardwick Hall, Father will at last have a clear field to sort things out. There's a hell of a lot to be done at Chatsworth. Father does not like the prospect of being there permanently in its present state. It will take some time before it can be really brought back to standard. As he is only in his mid-forties he will have plenty of time, which certainly suits me. I shan't have to worry about being stuck with the title for donkeys years to come, thank heaven. You and I have always been the best of pals. You've always said that you have never been disappointed that you were not the eldest."

Andrew replied, "I'm delighted that one day you'll be the next Duke and not me. For the time being, you being Lord Hartington and me Lord Burlington suits me fine."

"Are you still keen on the idea of going into publishing?" said Hartington.

"Yes, I've already hinted to Uncle Mac that I should like to. After all, he is the chairman of Macmillan Press – he should be able to fix it, although at the present time he seems more interested in politics – being in the government – perhaps one day he has visions of climbing to the top."

Their uncle, Harold Macmillan, the grandson of a Scottish crofter, had at an early age built up a flourishing publishing company, now one of the leaders in the industry. His ambitions were however elsewhere – he was a staunch member of the Conservative Party, already climbing up the political ladder.

Despite his humble beginning he married into the Devonshire family and became accepted by the establishment. In the post-war period he became British Prime Minister.

"Anyway," said Andrew, "it's all very well our having bright ideas for the future: the way things are going with this madman Hitler, we know where we shall be – in the army." They both grinned, lifted their glasses and said "Cheers!"

* * *

Life in London was, for Rose, just wonderful – far better than she could have ever imagined. She went everywhere, met everyone. She took Kathleen with her – she loved it too.

Kathleen's parents arranged for her to have a magnificent debutante coming-out party – the usual method of mothers launching their daughters into society – to start looking around the field for prospective suitable husbands. Kathleen was the belle of the ball – she had arrived.

On 25 July the family were invited to attend a royal garden party at Buckingham Palace. There was, of course, the usual large number of guests, but a private area was reserved for the favoured guests – which included the Kennedys. The King and Queen had passed by, nodding to their guests, when the Kennedys turned and were introduced to the party next to them – the Devonshires.

Kathleen turned and saw Bill Hartington smiling down on her. As if by instinct she knew this was the man she wanted to marry. They strolled off together, chatting as if they were old friends. When they were all about to depart he turned to her and, to her great delight, said, "We're going down to our place in Sussex for a few days for Goodwood – if I can fix it, would you like to come?"

She didn't know where Sussex was, she didn't know what Goodwood was, but there was no question – she would love to come.

Two days later the phone rang. Rose answered it. When she replaced the receiver she was all a-twitter. She burst into the lounge. "Joe, you'll never guess who that was on the phone – the Duchess of Devonshire.'

"Go on," he said. "What the devil did she want?"

"She rang up to say that they would like to invite Kathleen to their home in Sussex for a few days to go with them and Lord Hartington to the Goodwood Races – would we agree to her going?"

Joe grinned. "I bet you didn't say no."

"Of course I said she could go," said the delighted Rose.

A few days later Bill picked up Kathleen at the family home and in his small two-seater sports car they drove from the outskirts of London into the winding lanes of Sussex, travelling through the beautiful Ashdown Forest until they came to the seaside town of Eastbourne. Driving around the perimeter of the town, they turned off the road into the drive of the Devonshires' country mansion, Compton Place.

"The family came down yesterday," he said. "We shall be driving up to Goodwood each day – it'll take about an hour." She had been making a few enquires: it seemed that "going to Goodwood" meant to go to the special horse race meeting known as "Glorious Goodwood" – the most beautiful racecourse in Britain, situated in the midst of the Sussex Downs. Although not a royal meeting, this was the meeting that the upper crust made their own.

"I didn't know you had a house on the south coast, Bill. I thought your houses were all in the North of England."

"They all are except this one," he replied. As they drew up in front of the house she saw that it was a large Victorian type of mansion set in complete privacy in its own grounds. Although obviously spacious, it was not massive.

She was made most welcome by her hosts, the Duke and Duchess, and was installed in a large old-fashioned bedroom. At lunch she enjoyed the easy, friendly atmosphere which prevailed. "It's a lovely day, Bill," said the Duke. "Perhaps Kathleen would like you to show her around."

"I'd love that," she said, "but please, call me Kick – everyone calls me Kick."

"Bill and Kick – well, I haven't heard that before," he laughed.

They put on walking shoes and made their way to the rear of the house past the unused stables. She stopped to admire the beautiful rose garden, from which a large lawn sloped upwards to a wood. "There's a story about that wood," said Bill. "My great-great-grandfather, the second Earl of Buckingham, before he inherited the title from his uncle and became the seventh Duke, took a fancy to this area, bought and knocked down the old house which was on the site and built Compton Place virtually as it is today. He wanted complete privacy. This lawn was fairly flat – he could see houses of the village in the distance. He employed a great gang of labourers to dig up the land at the far end and build up a large artificial hill, which is lawn today. On the top he planted literally dozens of specimen trees, and now, as you can see, it now looks like a natural woodland. He also built this long flint wall all along the perimeter of the grounds to give complete privacy from the road."

They made their way to the front of the house and walked across the well-kept lawns. "The old boy was dead keen on forestry – just like my father is. He had all these trees, which are all specimen trees, imported especially from abroad. If you're not feeling tired, how would you like to walk to the top of the Downs? – it's a bit of a pull, but from there the views are well worth seeing." She readily agreed. They climbed the fence at the end of the lawns onto the golf course ahead of them.

"This is the Royal Eastbourne – we own all the land, except for a bit in the corner of the Downs in the distance, but of course we rent it to the club. At the beginning of the century, when golf was starting to become popular, the old Duke got the bug and they built a nine-hole course – he was the first Patron. Of course it's a full eighteen-hole course now. I'm a member, but I don't get down here very often to play. Father is the present Patron."

Crossing the golf course, they followed the path leading up to the top of the Downs – it was quite a trek. Walking along the crest they came to the top of the headland – Beachy Head. She was enthralled by the views. Below could be seen the elegant promenade of the town – the beaches, the pier, the smart bandstand, the line of bathing chalets – she could see the people swimming as the blue sea lapped the shore.

"If you look across the sea towards that headland there, you'll see two towns, Bexhill and Hastings, but past the pier in the distance you'll see a tower, one of the many along the South Coast which was one of those built when it was feared that Napoleon was going to invade England. Just past there is a bay – Pevensey Bay. Being an American, I don't suppose you've ever heard of it, but it was there in 1066 that William of Normandy landed with all his troops. There was a battle up on the hill beyond. He defeated the English King Harold, who was killed in the battle, and became William I, King of England. It's the one date in history that nearly everyone in England knows."

"Bill, I think it's delightful here, but how did your family come to be involved with this town?"

"Well, we were involved with it because we built it."

"You built it? I don't understand."

"Do you really want to know? It's quite a long story. Are you sure you won't be bored?"

"Of course I want to know. Let's sit down – you tell me." They made themselves comfortable on the grass.

"You see," he started, "the sixth Duke was a bachelor – by all accounts a bit of a lad – spent his life buying works of art and chasing women. When he died the whole of

Devonshire's estates and wealth was inherited by the nearest male relative, the second Earl of Burlington. Now he was already very rich: he had inherited from his grandfather several large properties and large areas of land in Kent and in this part of Sussex. So when he became the seventh Duke he became one of the wealthiest men in Britain, as well as owning Lismore in Ireland and the land there: he inherited the lot. We're talking about the 1830s, at which time Eastbourne was a small village. By all accounts, he was a very sober chap, very religious and devoted to his family. This was the time of the Industrial Revolution. He felt that he should use his wealth to help to build up Britain as a major manufacturing nation. He virtually built from scratch the town of Barrow in Furness, on the north-west coast, into a large manufacturing town.

"Way back, a spa named Bath, not far from Bristol, had been the gathering place of the British gentry. Well, the first Duke decided to build a spa to compete with it at Buxton in Derbyshire, not far from Chatsworth. He didn't really finish it, so the seventh Duke built it up very much like it is today, but it has never come up to Bath's standard. He was quite an astute chap: he bought lots of shares in the new industries which were springing up and greatly improved the finances of the estate. At that time there was a new innovation – towns were being built up by the sea for pleasure. He visited one or two resorts, in particular Brighton, which he didn't think much of. He didn't think any of them compared with those which were built in France. So when the railway was brought into Eastbourne in 1850, he decided that he would build up Eastbourne to become the home of wealthy people for leisure – to be the Empress of British watering places. He appointed a local builder named George Wallis to be his agent, and from the middle of the 1880s to the end of the century he poured money into the building of the town. You'll see when we go into town the wide, elegant tree-lined avenues and roads, the large Victorian houses into which the wealthy moved. He provided the money to buy the shares to enable the waterworks company and the gas company to be built, money to build the pier, and financed the building of the promenade. The Duke founded Eastbourne College and gave to the town a large area near the seafront to become Devonshire Park. When we go into town there's one thing you will notice – the avenues and roads are all named after the family – Devonshire Place, Burlington Place, Cavendish Avenue, Compton Road, Spencer Road and more. Of course there's Hartington Place – I think it's fair to say that the old boy made a very good job of making Eastbourne the Empress of Britain's watering places. God, you must be getting bored with all this."

"No, really I'm not," she replied, "I'm quite fascinated. The eighth Duke – he was your great-grandfather, wasn't he?"

"Yes. He was quite a character. He didn't get married until he was sixty. He didn't succeed to the title till he was fifty-eight; his father lived to a ripe old age. He was very much involved with politics all his life. He had a nickname in Parliament – Harty Tarty. By all accounts he was seen to be so lazy that not only was he always going to sleep on the front bench, he even went to sleep in the middle of his speeches. In actual fact he was a very astute old bird. He had several senior posts in the government. It looked at one time as if he would be Prime Minster, but he had a row with the then government led by Asquith, who was advocating Home Rule for Ireland. He didn't go for that at all – after all we own Lismore and all the land around it."

"How was it that he didn't marry until he was sixty?" she enquired.

"Well, it didn't mean that he didn't get around – he had a lifelong love affair with the Duchess of Manchester. No one seems to know what her husband thought of it. Behind his back she was known as the Double Duchess. Anyway, when Manchester died, they married. Meanwhile, it seems that he and his pals took their pleasures in the arms of a lady of the town known as 'Skittles'.'

"Of course, as he had no son, the title and everything had to pass to the nearest male heir – his nephew, Victor Cavendish, my grandfather. Come on, that's enough." They got to their feet and, holding hands, made their way back to the house. Kick was fascinated by what she heard. There was still so much she wanted to know about the background of the famous family of which she intended to be part.

7

The next morning they all travelled together in the family Rolls to Goodwood. The race meeting – "Glorious Goodwood" – far exceeded Kick's expectations. The whole show was organised by the Duke of Hamilton, who owned the land. He and the Duke of Devonshire were treated as top dogs and with due deference. The whole atmosphere was very different to those racecourses she had been taken to by her father in America. In the special enclosure reserved for the VIPs, each little clique had its own champagne party. Kick was very pleased with herself and the summer dresses she had been able to buy at short notice: she caused quite a stir.

The mothers of the debutantes, who were on the lookout for suitable husbands for their daughters, all wanted to meet this young American girl who had made such a hit with Lord Hartington. Surely this was just a passing affair – he was the most eligible of bachelors. The Devonshires always married within the titled clique. Of course, the girl's father, the American Ambassador, was alleged to be fabulously rich, but it was not the type of family you would expect a Devonshire to marry into. Kick felt that she was being well and truly looked over as they weighed up the opposition.

To her, it was all great fun. She and Bill argued as to

which horses to back, and to her great amusement at the end of the meeting she was a few pounds in hand, whilst Bill was in the red. The meeting ended far too soon, and travelling back to Compton Place on the last day Kick sighed – if only life was always like this.

After an early dinner that evening Kick thanked her hosts for such an enjoyable time. She enquired of the Duke, "You are so much involved with horse racing – do you own and race any horses yourself?"

"Oh yes," he replied. "I'm quite keen, but I only have a few, which are out with professional trainers. I should like to do more, but now that I have all the estates to supervise I haven't the time. If, later on, Bill starts taking over some of what's involved, I should like to be able to build up a string. My great-uncle, the old Duke, was quite an enthusiast. He always had a large number of horses in training."

* * *

After dinner the Duke and Duchess decided to drive back to their London home that evening. They would be there in less than two hours.

"Mary, what do you think of this business between Kick and Bill?" said the Duke.

"I like her very much," she replied, "but they are both very young. Bill's not yet twenty-one. She is certainly a very big improvement on some of the high flyers he's been around with. I don't suppose anything will come of it, although they seem very much taken with each other."

"What do you think of her family?" he enquired.

"I don't know. Her mother is amazing – she's had nine children and managed to keep her figure; she dresses very smartly; very capable of looking after herself and travelling around. The father – well, I don't know. I'm a bit sceptical. Of course, he has pots of money, but I'm not too happy with what I hear about his reputation in the States, and I'm not at all happy at the way he is supporting Chamberlain's appeasement policy, or his pro-Irish attitude. I don't want to be closely associated with him. Still, like you, I quite like Kick. We'll just have to let the affair run its course. I expect it will fade out."

* * *

Bill and Kick had decided to spend one more night at Compton Place before motoring back to London in his car.

"Mrs R, I'd like some more coffee," Bill called from the dining room across the hall to the kitchen. He had just finished his substantial breakfast. Gladys Rawlins and her husband, George, had run the household of Compton Place for as long as he could remember – he as butler, she as cook, employing extra staff as necessary. Often the family did not come down for long periods. Bill and his brother, Andrew, when young, used to sneak into the kitchen and pinch cakes from the larder. She issued dire threats that she would tell their father, but she never did. They kept the house and gardens in first-class condition. They were not overawed by the guests that their employers sometimes entertained. In 1934 George V and Queen Mary came to stay, and later the Duke and Duchess of York and their two young daughters visited. The Rawlins, like many other employees on the Duke's estates, stayed in their employ all their lives. Staff were never sacked. They were looked after when sick or in difficulties, and were not neglected in their old age – almost a feudal tradition.

“Thanks, Mrs R. Is Miss Kennedy coming down to breakfast, or is she having it in her room?”

“She’s already been down, Sir; she’s getting ready to go out. She said that she would like to go to Mass. She asked me if it was far to the nearest Roman Catholic church. I think she was going to ask you to take her there until I told her that it was only around the corner. I did right, didn’t I?”

“Of course you did, Mrs R,” he said. “Run up and tell her I’ll take her. I’ll just put on my things.”

Mrs Rawlins turned away with no further comment. They were both thinking along the same lines – a Roman Catholic church.

“Hello, Kick – how did you sleep?”

“Fine,” she said.

“Mrs R said you wanted to go to Mass. Our Lady of Ransom is only a stone’s throw away; I’ll walk you there,” he said.

“Thanks, Bill. Are you sure you don’t mind?”

They walked down the drive to the road, turned right and, after a short distance, came to a gate in the other side of the road leading to a large sports ground. “We’ll go through here,” he said.

“But it’s marked private.”

“That’s all right,” he replied, “this is the Saffrons sports ground – we own the freehold. The Saffrons cricket, football, croquet, hockey and bowls clubs play here. They lease the land from us. Father is the Patron of all the sections. The eighth Duke gave them a hundred-year lease in 1902. Of course, the rent they pay is peanuts.”

They walked across the grounds to the far gate, and there across the road, was the church.

“Bill,” she said, “I know that you’re not RC, but I’m sure

that you would be interested to sit in on one of our services."

"Good Lord," said Bill, "didn't you know that the family fortune was founded at the time of Henry VIII when he broke away from Rome and founded the Church of England? The Pope wouldn't agree to give him a divorce from his first wife. My ancestor, William Cavendish, got the job of transferring all the wealth of the RC churches, priories, nunneries – everything and all their land to the Church of England. He was very efficient, but you can guess he wasn't very popular. He didn't do badly on the deal for himself; in fact the family fortune was founded on his efforts. The family have, of course, been staunch members and leaders of the Protestant Church of England ever since. Crikey, if I ever attended a Roman Catholic church service there would be a hell of a row. You understand, don't you? When you're through, walk back across the Saffrons. If anyone stops you, tell them you're my guest. Bye."

Sitting in the church, Kick's thoughts were far away from the service. The last few days had made up her mind: she wanted to marry Bill – to be Lady Hartington, the future Duchess of Devonshire.

What she had just heard had raised an issue which she had previously considered of little importance. She knew that on no account would her father and mother allow her to marry outside the Catholic faith. She had vaguely thought that Bill might agree to become RC, but after what she had just heard that seemed impossible. One day she would have to face up to the problem, but in any event she was not going to give up Bill.

8

So much for Hitler's word: throughout the months of January and February 1939 there were reports of more movements of Hitler's forces in central Europe.

Chamberlain's position was becoming untenable. Whilst he was being pressed by the Cliveden Set to maintain peace with Hitler, Winston Churchill, who was not in the government, was loud in his condemnation of him for not standing up to Hitler. He was strongly supported by Anthony Eden. Churchill was getting inside information which could have only come from official sources, and leading personnel in the forces were coming out strongly in favour of his views.

Without warning, on 15 March Hitler invaded Czechoslovakia. Britain and France had made a half promise to support the Czechs if they were attacked, but they took no action – they did not have the means. Despite the heroism of the tiny Czech army, they were overwhelmed in a matter of days. They had no alternative but to capitulate.

In Britain, public opinion was swinging against Chamberlain. Churchill was being heralded as the man who had been right all along – the policy of appeasement over the last few years had been wrong from the outset. The public were nervous. It seemed that war was coming nearer and nearer – it seemed inevitable.

Chamberlain's policy was now in tatters. All his hopes had come to nothing. Peace could not be made with a mad dictator. He immediately warned Hitler that if he made any further military moves in Europe it would mean war. To add strength to his stand, Britain and France guaranteed the frontiers of Poland – brave words.

Joe Kennedy was now in a most difficult position. His argument that Britain should negotiate peace with Hitler had proved to be quite wrong. His reports to Washington made things quite clear – America must not intercede in any way in Europe.

To support their undertaking to Poland, Britain and France felt that they had one trump card – the military alliance between France and the Soviet Union. Both countries pledged that if one was engaged in war, the other would immediately take military action to support it. Surely Hitler could not possibly risk a war on all sides. The countries in Europe outside Hitler's domain were now trying desperately to re-equip and modernise their forces.

FDR's scheme, which had been welcomed by all his colleagues, to get Kennedy out of their hair by sending him to London, was turning sour. He had to do something to clip Joe's wings. It was most important that he should keep even closer in touch with the British Government. At the same time, he would have to keep Joe reasonably happy with the responsibilities of being Ambassador.

Even after the invasion of Czechoslovakia, Joe's policy was appeasement at any price. He created a terrible row when, on being invited to address a meeting of businessmen in London, he stated that the US and Britain should again try and negotiate with Hitler on all outstanding matters; he was sure that Hitler would cooperate. The press made the speech headline news. He was howled at from all sides. Jews in America were now realising the dreadful and inhuman treatment that fellow Jews were being subjected to by the Nazis. The Jewish lobby in Washington complained bitterly to the President, who had to try to placate everyone on both sides of the Atlantic. He stated publicly that the views expressed by Ambassador Kennedy were not the official views of the US Government.

Joe realised that he had overstepped the mark: he stated that he had been misunderstood, that everyone would agree that every effort must be made to prevent war – a war which he was sure nobody wanted. In an attempt to save face, Joe put forward a scheme for which he sought the support of all nations; that hundreds of thousands of Jews living in Germany should be transported to other countries throughout the world. it was such a crack-brained scheme that Jews everywhere resented it. It did not do anything to improve Joe's image. They held the whole idea up to ridicule. It did, if anything, weaken the whole idea of appeasement.

Jews in every corner of the world were worrying where the horror of Hitler's treatment of their people would end. Over the centuries, Jews had been forced to leave their native land to find a life elsewhere, where they could live peacefully. They had been accepted by host countries as citizens – had achieved high office – contributed greatly to the wealth and arts of the nations of which they were part. The scheme suggested by Kennedy was absurd. The Jews in Germany were citizens – true Germans – proud to be Germans. Surely this man Hitler must realise the great value to the German nation the Jewish population contributed? Not so: unfortunately the stories of their treatment were as nothing to the reality – the horrors of the concentration camps, the gas chambers, the extermination of thousands and thousands of them in the near future – it was too horrible to consider that such treatment by humans beings of other human beings be possible.

9

"What are we going to do about Joe?" FDR, seated at his desk, was facing the Secretary of State.

"It beats me: I just don't know," said Hull.

"I've just had a note from him," continued Roosevelt, "to say that he intends taking leave. He wants the family to visit Rome with him. Tell me who have we got in the embassy in London who knows the ropes; someone who has been there some time?"

"Well, there's Charlie Ruston, the First Secretary."

"What do you know about him?"

"He's been in the Diplomatic Corps since he left University. He's in his forties. He's been abroad for most of his time, in London for about six years. He knows the ropes."

"I suppose, then, that he knows, and is well known to, his opposite members in the other embassies?"

"I've met him a few times. He struck me as a quiet sort of chap. I understand he's very efficient," said Hull.

"Is he married?" asked FDR.

"Very much so, I believe. He has a flat in Knightsbridge. I gather he and his wife prefer a quiet life. Of course, they have to attend all the usual parties. They have two teenaged sons who are at school over here. But what's this all about?"

"I'll write to Joe saying that I hope that he and the family have a good holiday. I'll say that, in view of the tense situation in Europe, he will want the embassy to be as fully staffed as possible whilst he is away, and suggest that he sends Ruston on leave now so that he can be back whilst he is on holiday. I'm sure that he'll buy that."

"Suppose he does," queried Hull, "what's the purpose of it all?"

"As soon as Joe has had the message, I want you to phone Ruston in the evening at his flat. Tell him that we wish him to take his leave over here. He and his wife can come over and back on the *Queen Elizabeth.* When he's here, I want you to see him. Joe is not to know that you phoned."

"OK," said Hull, "I'll lay it on, then perhaps you'll tell me what it's all about."

"Oh, I will, I'll tell you all right," replied FDR.

* * *

Charles Ruston entered his Knightsbridge flat, hung up his coat and hat and called out "I'm home." His wife, in the kitchen preparing the evening meal, replied, "Hello dear," the usual greeting on his return from the embassy. Going into the lounge, he prepared a couple of gin and tonics – their usual tipple – and relaxed in his chair. Clare came in, leaned over and gave him her usual greeting kiss. The flat was a little over a mile from the embassy. He diligently walked there in the mornings for the exercise but, packing up about six, came home by taxi.

"Did you have a good day?" she said as she often did, "You look a bit whacked."

"It depends what you mean by a good day – you may think so."

"What do you mean?" she said.

"Joe Kennedy called me into his office today. You know what he's like; if he's fixing something to suit himself, he's all gushing and friendly." Clare groaned – she didn't like Kennedy.

"He told me that he was taking the family to the continent for June and July – he's fixed that with Washington. He will also be making some diplomatic calls. They've agreed, but stipulated that, in view of the problems in Europe, the other senior members of the staff must not be away at the same time. They'd checked and found that I was due to be on leave at the same time."

"You're not going to tell me that those damn Kennedys have managed to get our leave cancelled? It's not damn right. You know that the embassy operates well whether he's there or not – it's always properly staffed. You'll have to tell them you will not stand for it. It's all arranged for us to go home and see the boys."

"Hold on, hold on – listen: instead of going on leave after July, we're going now. They've booked a suite for us on the *Queen Elizabeth,* sailing from Southampton on Saturday."

"Saturday – why, it's Wednesday now; I can't possibly be ready to leave by Saturday. Have we really got to go? Why such short notice? It will be great to see the boys sooner, but the weather in Long Island is better in July than May. What's it all about?" she said.

"I don't know what it's all about. Not only are we having a suite on the *Queen Elizabeth* both ways, all expenses paid, but we can bring the boys across here in July, all expenses paid. Why am I getting this VIP treatment? I just can't understand it."

"Well, Charlie, if we've got to go, we've got to go. I'll

dash round and do my shopping tomorrow, get my hair done – it'll cost you – you'll have to do the packing. God – the meal will burn." She rushed off into the kitchen.

Over the meal they discussed all the arrangements that had to be made, and after they had cleaned away he settled down in the lounge, waiting for her to bring in the coffee. The phone rang.

"I'll get it," he called. He picked up the receiver. A voice said, "I have a long-distance call for Mr Charles Ruston. Is that Mr Ruston speaking, please?"

"Yes, yes."

"Hold the line please." His heart jumped – was anything wrong with the boys? "That is Mr Ruston in person?"

"Yes."

"I'm putting you through to the Secretary of State, Sir."

What the hell was the Secretary of State phoning him for, and why at his flat?

"Hello, Charles, how are you?"

"I'm fine, Sir – and you?"

"It's a long time since we met. How are things at the embassy? I'm sure that things are running smoothly now that Ambassador Kennedy has settled in."

"Yes Sir, things are running very smoothly."

"I thought I would give you a call to say it's a pity you have had to alter your leave arrangements. You are coming over this weekend OK, I presume?"

"Oh yes, Sir. It's very short notice; my wife will be running around getting ready to go," said Charles.

"I guess so. There's something I wanted to say. When you're over here, I want you to phone my secretary and make a date for you to come and have a talk with me in Washington. Is that OK? Now, this is most important: I do not want you to tell anyone, and that includes Mr

Kennedy, that we're having this meeting – no one," said Hull.

"I understand. I'm to tell no one. Is that official?"

"That is official. You tell no one. Well, I hope you both have a good trip. My regards to your wife. Goodbye."

"Goodbye, Sir."

He replaced the receiver feeling stunned. What was that all about? Clare, coming in from the kitchen with the coffee, enquired, "Who was that, dear?"

"Oh, that was long-distance – the Secretary of State, Cordell Hull."

"What the devil did he want? Why did he phone you here?"

"He phoned to say that while I'm on leave I'm to contact his secretary and make a date to see him in Washington but, and this is it, no one, and I mean no one, including Kennedy, is to be told that I'm to see him; I haven't the slightest idea what it's all about. I don't like the smell of it. But listen, Clare, it's official – no one must know, not a soul. I know that I can trust you."

She gave him a hug. "You can trust me."

10

Rose loved entertaining and giving dinner parties. She usually did these in style at the embassy or one of the high-class hotels, such as Claridges. Occasionally, at Joe's request, she arranged dinner at home for his guests when he wanted to see someone unofficially.

"Joe, I don't like the way things are going at all." The speaker was Pat O'Donnell, the Irish Ambassador to Britain. They were sitting in Joe's den, after an enjoyable dinner, with their coffee and brandies. Rose and O'Donnell's wife were taking their coffee in the lounge.

"The other day, I was entertained to lunch at the German Embassy. You know the Ambassador – he's a likeable old boy, one of the old school. Well, after lunch we adjourned to his office. We were joined by a Colonel Braun. The conversation over lunch had been all small talk, but when we settled down in his office this chap took over. He was a bumptious bastard. Apparently, he was very high up in the German Foreign Office in Berlin. He started off by saying that the last thing Hitler wanted was to quarrel with Britain. Nobody wanted war. Hitler was very concerned that, under pressure from people like Churchill, Chamberlain's peace policy was being undermined. There appeared to be a very strong anti-Nazi lobby in Britain. If the warmongers in Britain prevailed and the unthinkable happened and there was a war, then Ireland would be in a very precarious position. He stated that, in view of the great strength of the German forces, Britain and France could not possibly hold out against them.

"He had been instructed by Von Ribbentrop to ask me to convey to De Valera Germany's goodwill toward Ireland and our desire that Ireland would in no way be involved with Germany's quarrel with Britain."

"That's fine, Pat. I'm really pleased to hear that," said Joe.

"I'm afraid that's not all; he said that Hitler would observe Ireland's neutrality and after the end of hostilities he would see that Ireland would achieve her dream of a united Ireland, including Ulster. But – and here's the rub, Joe – Hitler wants an agreement that if there is a war he would be allowed to establish depots and stores for the servicing of U-boats along the west coast of Ireland. Joe, this is dynamite. I've sent a report to De Valera but haven't yet had a reply. I cannot for one moment see that Britain would stand for that. Ireland would become a battlefield – there would be a civil war. I felt that you should know off the record.

"According to Churchill, Hitler still fears the superiority of the British Navy surface ships, so he is building a large fleet of U-boats. Bases on our west coast would give them a free hand to attack shipping in the Atlantic; as well as the British Navy, the merchant ships bringing in food and supplies. In the last war, in 1917, the Germans, by doing this, nearly brought Britain to the point of starvation. Bases on our west coast would be invaluable to him." O'Donnell sat back, sipped his whisky and waited for Joe's reaction.

"This is bloody terrible. As you say, Britain would not stand for it. I can report this to Washington, but if I do there will be a terrible outcry among the Irish Americans, and the backlash may bring in more support in the States for Britain to stand firm against Hitler. There's only one thing for us to do: plead for Britain to try again for a negotiated peace with Hitler, despite what's happened to Czechoslovakia. Have you any idea what De Valera will do?" said Joe.

"After he had my report he phoned me to say that, other than telling yourself, I was to keep the issue under wraps. He thinks that Hitler knows that he cannot be committed at the present time and that what he wants has put us on the spot, so De Valera says he can only play for time."

Full of foreboding, they left Joe's den and joined the ladies.

* * *

Sitting in his office at the embassy next morning, Joe could not make up his mind as to what action he should take on the news. If he reported to Washington on information received, he knew the upheaval it would cause. On the other hand, if he kept it to himself and it came out at a later date, he would really be for it. He decided he, like De Valera, would play for time. To cover himself he wrote a brief account, placed in a folder and marked it "Strictly private", for his personal attention on his return from holiday. He hid the folder beneath a pile of documents at the bottom of the safe.

11

The Rustons had an excellent trip to New York on the *Queen Elizabeth*: the accommodation, the food, the entertainment, the dancing – Clare enjoyed every minute of it.

As the ship docked, they were thrilled to see their two boys waving to them from the quayside. Clare's brother had driven down to take them back to her widowed mother's large house in Long Island, where they would spend their leave, their own house having been let. After being duly installed, they said that they would be spending a day or two in Washington to look up old friends. Shortly after their arrival, Charles duly phoned Cordell Hull's secretary and made a date for his appointment, and he and Clare took the train down to Washington.

"Pleased to see you, Charles," said the Secretary of State. "Did you have a good trip?"

"Fine thanks, Sir. The arrangements were excellent."

"Well, I suppose you're wondering what this is all about."

"Yes, Sir, I sure am," replied Charles.

"It's very delicate, Charles. You know what an excellent job Senator Kennedy is doing in London. He has very strong views and, as you know, his main concern is that there is not a war, but if there is, we must not be implicated. This is something we must all hope and pray for. The problem is that what he is doing is not appreciated by the British Government. They feel – quite correctly – that if Hitler were to have his way, he would control the whole of Europe, including Britain. Then what would be our position? Where would America stand in the world? Could we line up with Hitler? Of course not. If there is a war, we intend to stay neutral but, let's face it, underneath it all it is in our interests to support Britain. How can we do that in London if our Ambassador is acting otherwise?

"We must therefore be in a position in London to negotiate matters of great national concern with the British Government. We must know Britain's moods. We must pass on information to them which will help them – so we want you at the embassy to be the contact man with them. You must be the go-between. You have, as First Secretary, control of the diplomatic bag; you can secure and despatch secret information which is essential to both sides. I have already cleared this with Lord Halifax; we have agreed that you will, no doubt, have a personal contact with staff at their Foreign Office. If you have someone there you can trust implicitly, you are to approach them privately and make the necessary arrangements; if you haven't, Halifax will appoint someone."

"Sir, before you go any further," butted in Ruston, "where does Mr Kennedy stand in all this?"

"As I said before, the position is delicate. The arrangement is a direct contact between your contact with the British and yourself with this Office."

"In other words, Mr Kennedy is to be kept in the dark – he is not to know what I'm doing."

"You must realise that we cannot afford the publicity which would be caused if we brought Mr Kennedy home;

at the same time, we must appear to be neutral, but behind the scenes we have to support the British," said Hull.

Ruston said, "I don't like it – not at all. May I have the instructions in writing?"

"No – this is official. You won't have it in writing. You must realise the problems we are faced with."

"Then if Mr Kennedy finds out, I'm the fall guy," said Ruston.

"Then you mustn't let him find out, must you?" said Hull. "Now, tell me, do you have a contact at the British Foreign Office who would act as your opposite number? Someone like yourself who will act for them?"

"Yes, one of them is a friend of mine; we play bridge together. But he may not want to do it," said Ruston.

"Oh yes, he will – it will be cleared at top level. Their Foreign Office are all for it; they feel that they have no friend in Ambassador Kennedy. This arrangement must be kept strictly secret. It certainly must not get known by the Nazis." Hull picked up the phone and told the operator to get the number he had previously instructed. The phone rang. He picked up the receiver and turned to Charles. "This is for you."

"For me? Why for me?" said Charles as he took the receiver.

"Is that Charles Ruston? I'm pleased to say hello, Mr Ruston, this is the President." Charles nearly dropped the receiver. "I just wanted to say that I'm sure that you appreciate the importance of the job I have asked the Secretary of State to arrange. Mr Kennedy is a great friend of mine, and this arrangement doesn't mean that we aren't happy with the job he's doing for us in London, but the next few months are going to bring some tricky problems. The arrangement must not, of course, interfere with the Kennedy's normal duties as our Ambassador. I'm sure I can rely on you to handle everything diplomatically and without any difficulty. Goodbye, and good luck."

Charles felt stunned. "Now are you satisfied?" Charles nodded. "I shall be contacting the British Foreign Office to tell them you are arranging the contact. Thanks for your cooperation. I'm sure you'll handle everything admirably. Have a good leave."

They shook hands, and Charles left the office completely dazed.

* * *

On his return to London at the end of his leave, he found that the fear of war was everywhere.

He phoned George Smithers and asked if he and his wife would come to play bridge. "I'll check with the social secretary," said George. "That's OK – we'll be with you tomorrow evening. Did you have a good leave?"

"I'll tell you all about it tomorrow."

After setting up the drinks Charles said, "George, before we start to play I want to have a word with you; let's go into the den."

George's wife, Mary, guessed, "Secret, is it?"

"Oh, let them get on with it," said Clare.

After Charles had spelled it out to George, he wanted clearance – he had never previously been involved in intrigue. It was so high-level that he didn't doubt what Charles had told him. He agreed to be party to the scheme, providing he had clearance from the top. He was all for closer contact with America in the present crisis.

"You say that Washington have already advised our

Foreign Office of the scheme, and that I'm now to see Lord Halifax personally to OK the arrangement? I'll try to do that tomorrow. If he officially OKs it, then I'm in – but I'm not putting my job on the line without his authority. I'll be in touch as soon as I've seen him." They joined their wives.

The next morning he phoned through to the Foreign Secretary's private secretary. "I'm Smithers, Head of the US Section," he said. "I should like to see the Foreign Secretary on a delicate matter regarding the United States. Would you ask him to see me?"

She came back to him. "He will see you at three o'clock."

* * *

"So you are to be the contact," said Lord Halifax. He had met Smithers previously. "I've heard from Washington and I've had a word with the Prime Minister; he is in full agreement. But this arrangement is only to be used for highly confidential matters between Washington and ourselves. Routine matters take their normal course. It is essential, Smithers, that no details of this arrangement seep out. It must not be known to Mr Kennedy. If it were not for his extreme pro-Irish, anti-British views it would not be necessary. I understand that your contact in the American Embassy is named Ruston, and that you know him quite well."

"Oh yes, we are good friends," said Smithers. "We meet socially."

"That's fine, so that any information which we want kept secret can be passed between you without anyone suspecting any official contact," continued Halifax. "I don't like these kinds of political intrigues, but I'm sure you will handle the matter very well – good day."

"Good day, Sir." Smithers made his way back to his own office. As a senior civil servant, he was not used to this kind of undercover activity.

12

Kathleen had written to Bill, who was with his family at Chatsworth. She was not at all happy that she would not be able to see him for about a month. She had to go on holiday with her family to Italy. They would be away from the middle of June to about the end of July. It was to be something special – her father was to meet the King of Italy and Mussolini, and the family were to have a private audience with the Pope – she had to go.

Bill phoned as soon as he heard. He had not told her previously, but a great party was to be held at Chatsworth to celebrate his coming of age – it was going to be really something. He wanted her to be there – couldn't she fix it?

There was a terrific family row. The family were all assembled for dinner when Kick turned to her father and declared, "I am not going to Rome, I am going to Bill's twenty-first birthday party at Chatsworth." All conversation stopped.

"Listen to me, girl," said Joe. "All members of this family have been honoured with a private audience with His Holiness the Pope – when I say all members of the family that includes you. What do you expect me to say? We are all honoured to attend except my daughter Kathleen, she's going to a birthday party? Of course not. You will be coming with us – that is final."

"But don't you know what this means to me?" cried Kick. "It means that I shall be seen as Bill's girlfriend – I shall be accepted as a possible fiancée. I shall be part of his circle; that's what I want to be, that's why I want to and must go to his party."

"Where the devil is this leading us?" said Joe. "Do you really think that there is a possibility of you marrying Hartington? You know that as Roman Catholics, members of the true church, we abide by the rules – we do not marry outside our faith. I can't see Hartington agreeing to become a Roman Catholic. If you did get a dispensation it would be conditional that any children be brought up in the Roman Catholic faith – can you see the Devonshires agreeing to that? Of course not. That's settled – you come with us, Kick." She fled from the room.

"You know, Pa," Joe Junior said, "this family audience with the Pope should give us good publicity with the folks at home."

"That's beside the point," said Joe, "quite beside the point." As he left the room, Joe Junior and Jack turned to each other and grinned broadly – they knew when it came to good publicity Joe would not miss a trick.

The audience with the Pope was, for Rose, one of the great events of her life. The family, the ladies dressed in black, the men in dark suits, were escorted through the great St Peter's Cathedral, flanked by well-fed Cardinals dressed in their black robes and scarlet skull caps, to the Pope's private apartments. He had been well briefed. He complimented them on all the work and support that they did for the Church in America. He greatly admired the efforts that Joe was making in helping to maintain peace; he too prayed daily that there would be no war. He blessed them all – a most moving occasion, a great day for the Kennedys.

Joe and Rose were presented to King Victor of Italy who, together with the Queen, tried hard to keep up the traditions of royalty when, of course, they were mere puppets, kept in power by the Fascist dictator Mussolini. They were given the VIP treatment.

Joe Kennedy made his official call on Mussolini and was given a real state red carpet welcome.

"Mr Kennedy," said the Duce, "I am delighted to welcome you personally to our country and I should like you to carry to your President our greetings, our friendship and our best wishes. I should like you to inform him how much the people of Italy value the happy cooperation and relationship which exist between our two nations."

Joe responded in the same tone on behalf of the President of the USA. He had been ushered into a magnificent state reception room, and seated next to Mussolini on a raised dais, looking down on an assembly of Generals, Admirals and air force chiefs all bedecked with medals and insignias.

"Mr Kennedy, we should have liked you to have had more time to travel around our beautiful county," said the Duce. "We have over the last decade or so through our present single party government of which I am proud to be the leader, been able to unite all the small states and interests into one nation that has taken its rightful place in the nations of the world, and we have built up a very strong military, naval and air force to ensure the defence of our country from whatever source. Our critics say that our single government Fascist Party is a dictatorship – this is nonsense. We have done so much for the country and we know what is best for our people."

Joe tried to lead the conversation on to a wider field.

"There is, as you know, great concern throughout Europe at the present policies of the German Government," he said.

"This is pure nonsense," said the Duce. "Adolf Hitler is a friend. He used many of my ideas to assist him in forming his Party. Look what he has achieved for Germany. I understand that there are rumours that the Jews in Germany are being badly treated – this I find hard to believe. In Italy we have a considerable number of Jewish citizens and they have all the benefits of the state, the same as the rest of the population. There is no discrimination against them in any way."

Joe asked, "If, and I sincerely hope that it never happens, war were to break out in Europe, in view of your friendship with Hitler, would you feel that you were duty bound to support him?"

Mussolini glared at him. "I am the head of the Italian people, and I will take what action I feel right to protect their interests. If there is war in Europe it will not be of Hitler's making. Just because they do not like his method of government they threaten him with war, despite all his efforts to negotiate with them. Do they not realise how strong militarily he is? It would be crazy for them to start such a war. I would not be prepared to be involved in such a conflict – the consequences would be horrendous. I am concerned with protecting the interests of Italy. I am more than pleased to hear that you personally are doing all you can to ensure that in the event of war, America will not allow itself to be drawn in. I understand that throughout America the population as a whole do not want to be involved. Britain would of course make every effort it could to bring in America. It is fortunate that you are standing against such pressure – may I wish you every success in your campaign for peace."

Mussolini gave him an effusive farewell, strutting around in his flashy, black Fascist uniform. He was escorted out by his equally flashily attired yes-man – his son-in-law, Count Ciano. Joe was pleased with his visit. He had no illusions. He would report back to Washington. They should not trust Mussolini as far as they could throw him.

13

The coming of age party for Lord Hartington at Chatsworth was indeed a great event. There were no less than 2,800 guests – from some of the greatest names and members of the aristocracy in Britain, right down to the most lowly paid employees on the estates, members of the local churches and villages. It was a return to the feudal patronage of the past. Chatsworth had been dolled up to give it a resemblance to its former glory. It was a party that would be remembered by all who attended. It was as if it heralded the end of an era. Indeed, for the Devonshires it was the end of an era – there would never be a party like that again.

With the Ambassador on holiday, Charles Ruston's new role posed no immediate problems; he knew that these would arise on Kennedy's return. However, he had to see if Kennedy was free to address a meeting of the Anglo-Irish Society in September and to check with his appointments diary. He assumed that this was in his safe: only he had the keys. Sorting through the contents, looking for the diary, he came across the folder marked for Kennedy's attention on his return.

He opened the folder and was completely shattered. Why ever had Joe not got in touch with Washington following his discussion with Pat O'Donnell? Did he not realise what this information would mean to the British? Did he not, could he not, imagine what their reaction would be when they learned that Hitler was trying to do a deal with de Valera, that in the event of war, Germany would be allowed to have submarine bases on the west coast of Ireland. This facility would be disastrous to the shipping in the Atlantic. If the deal went through... What could Ruston do? Damn it! They might have to consider invading Ireland to prevent the bases being used. He must get the information back to Washington – it was dynamite.

He copied the report himself, replaced the original in the folder and placed it back in the safe exactly where he had found it. In view of its importance, he wrote personally to Cordell Hull:

> Dear Secretary of State
>
> I am so concerned at the contents of the enclosed report that I feel it must have your personal attention. I have not discussed it or shown it to anyone. It is not my practice to snoop into the Ambassador's private papers, but he is away at present and I had, on this occasion, to check a date in his diary which is kept in his safe, to which only he and I have the key. As I looked inside I saw the folder marked for his attention on his return. I am sending this to you in the diplomatic bag, as I fear for the consequences. Please let me have your instructions.

The next day his phone rang. He lifted the receiver.

"Ruston? This is Cordell Hull. This is a closed line, are you OK to receive at your end?"

"Yes, Sir," he said.

"You did a good job getting hold of this. The President and I are both very concerned. We have decided to take no action at this end at present, but will sit tight to see what transpires. Firstly, under no circumstances when he returns must Joe know that we have seen the file. Can you take another copy of it?"

"Yes."

"OK. Then, as soon as possible, meet your contact at the British FO and hand it over, telling him that we have obtained it from one of our agents. Do not mention Joe. Say we wish it to be handed personally to Halifax. He is to tell him that we are not involved and are taking no action. Well done. Goodbye."

Ruston phoned Smithers.

"George, I must see you. Meet me without fail, usual place, same time, when you leave the office."

"Sorry, old boy. No can do. We are off to a cocktail party, then out to dinner."

"Sorry, this is a must – we have to meet."

"I shall be in the dog-house with Mary. I'll blame you, Ruston."

They met as arranged. Ruston handed over the file and passed on the instructions he had received from Cordell Hull. He gave him the perfect gist of the report, swearing him to secrecy – it must be in the hands of Halifax at the earliest.

Smithers was relieved when he arrived at his office next morning with a copy of the file safely in his pocket. He phoned through with a request to see Lord Halifax urgently. He was ushered into the Foreign Secretary's office: Halifax, wearing his usual sour expression, nodded for him to sit down.

"Well, what's so urgent?" he asked.

Ruston handed the file to him. "This has come direct from Mr Cordell Hull via my contact, Sir, not through the normal channels of the American Embassy." Halifax did not like this cloak and dagger business. He opened the file and was aghast.

"Have you seen this?" he asked Smithers.

"No, Sir," replied Smithers, "but I have been given a brief outline of the contents. My instructions were that it must be handed to you personally."

"How many people have seen this file – do you know?" said Halifax.

"I understand only Mr Cordell Hull, my contact at the embassy, myself and now you, Sir.'

"Is Kennedy involved in this, do you know?"

"Not to my knowledge, Sir," said Smithers.

"Under no circumstances is any of this to leak out, you understand? I must discuss this privately with the Prime Minister as soon as possible. I will be in touch with you if you are to be involved further."

Two days later he was called in to see Halifax.

"This report, as you can imagine, has caused considerable concern and we are very pleased to have seen it. However, issues of great importance have just been reported and the contents of this report fit into the general pattern. At this stage we shall not take any direct action. We have very disconcerting news coming out of Germany and Russia. Through your contact send a message to Cordell Hull saying how much we appreciate that he has brought this to our notice."

* * *

The Kennedy family really enjoyed their holiday in Italy, seeing the sights of Rome, Florence, Pisa, Venice;

wherever they went, they received VIP treatment. It was all very interesting. Kick being the only objector – she wanted to have been at Chatsworth. They decided that before going home they would spend some time in Paris. As far as Rose was concerned, Paris was her scene – she loved Paris.

While they were there they were, of course, entertained at the American Embassy. After attending an official function, the American Ambassador asked Joe to join him in his private office.

"Joe," he said, "I am most worried at the news we are getting about troop movements in Germany – they are being moved towards the Polish border. Britain is calling on France and Russia, who are bound by treaty with them, to stand firm and support them in their demand that Hitler halts this move. The trouble is that the French Government are so weak and divided. Their sleazy Prime Minister, Pierre Laval, is trying every trick to sit on the fence. My information is that the French army is completely old-fashioned and badly equipped – it would be hopeless against the tanks and modern military hardware that the Germans could put against them in the field – and I don't think Britain would be any match for them either."

'Where do we stand in all this?" asked Joe. "We don't want America to become involved in this bloody mess."

"I quite agree," replied his colleague. "We must make our position clear from the outset that we are not prepared to take sides. It seems that Laval is telling everyone that if there were a war, France would be safe behind the Maginot Line – I think that is a pipe dream."

"Have you told Washington of the position?" asked Joe.

"Yes, they know the score. They are under pressure from Britain to declare their support against Hitler, but as you know, the vast majority of Americans do not wish to be involved in a war in Europe and so the official policy is that we remain neutral."

Joe returned to his hotel. The news was most disconcerting. It seemed that all attempts to come to a peaceful agreement with Hitler were a waste of time. If there was going to be a war, one thing was paramount, and he would do all he could to prevent America being involved in the conflict.

As he returned to the hotel he was given a message marked "Most urgent". He was to return to London immediately; the family could follow.

Reports had been received in Washington that the German Ambassador, Von Ribbentrop, had been seen in Moscow. He had been known to have had a meeting with Stalin. There were all sorts of rumours flying around as to why, in view of the known hatred between Nazism and Communism, he should be there. On 12 August the news broke. it was almost impossible to believe – Germany and Russia had signed a non-aggression pact. They would not wage war against each other. The Franco-Russian pact was worthless; the Russians had torn it up.

Hitler was beside himself with joy. He called a meeting of his cabinet and held forth: "I have had the most wonderful news," he cried. "Our colleague, Von Ribbentrop, has just returned from Russia. He has signed on our behalf and with my full agreement a pact with Stalin that if we decide to attack Poland from the west, he will attack them from the east and we will divide the country between us. You see what this means? We can now go ahead with our plans and I shall be issuing orders immediately. The great news is, of course, that if Britain and France threaten us with war if we invade Poland, then Russia would not support them: the military non-aggression pact they had with

Russia no longer exists. We owe a great debt of gratitude to Von Ribbentrop for pulling off this wonderful coup." He was cheered to the echo.

At the party, only one voice was raised showing any concern; this was Goebbels, the diminutive Minister of Propaganda.

"Can we really trust the Russians?" he asked.

"Trust the Russians?" replied Hitler. "Of course we can't trust the Russians. They hate us just like we hate them and all Communists. They have only signed this pact to play for time – their forces are in a hopeless state. Oh no, we don't trust them; one day, in the not-too-distant future, when we've come to terms with France and Britain on our terms, we shall have to deal with them."

The news, when received in London and Paris, caused great concern. The whole strategy of containing Hitler was in disarray. It was beyond anyone's dreams that Germany could, to all intents and purposes, join forces with Russia. When it came to honouring pledges, there seemed little to choose between Hitler and Stalin.

The signing of the pact put Britain and France in an impossible position. When they guaranteed Poland's frontiers, they had relied on Russia's support. Now, if Hitler invaded Poland, they had to decide – would they honour their word? Hitler did not think they would.

14

The threat of war had an immediate effect on the lives of the Devonshires. Bill and Andrew had been called up and had joined their units in the Coldstream Guards. The Duke, on the death of his father, had started a programme to renovate Chatsworth, Hardwick Hall and his other properties, but that was all halted; the government, having seen the dreadful effects of the bombing of open cities, had drawn up a list of large houses in the countryside to which children could be evacuated for safety, away from cities and towns. Chatsworth, Hardwick Hall and other houses owned by the Duke were on the list. All the valuables in the houses – works of art, pictures, silver, valuable books were all packed up and stored away in places of safety.

The Duke, before he inherited the title, was a keen politician. He had held for the Conservatives the parliamentary seat of West Derbyshire. He would have liked to have been involved in the war effort but his activities were now limited to the House of Lords.

* * *

Hitler wasted no time – it had, of course, been planned from the outset. In the middle of August he invaded Poland. The Polish Army put up a gallant defence but to no avail. The German Air Force mercilessly bombed defenceless Warsaw; it was in flames. The Poles' position was hopeless.

Hitler was cock-a-hoop; how could Britain hope to honour its commitment to Poland? They would have to stand aside. But his euphoria did not last long. He called his High Command and produced the message he had received from Chamberlain. He had been waiting to hear that Britain and France were now prepared to meet him to agree, on his terms, to a peaceful agreement. He was prepared to agree that he would only stand by his agreement with Russia as long as it was in the interest of all that Communism be curtailed.

"You assured me that Britain would never fight." He turned to Von Ribbentrop. He was tired – amazed. The message he had received from Chamberlain was final: unless he removed all his forces from Poland by 1 September, then Britain and France would honour their pledge to come to the aid of that country. He could not conceive that they would be so crazy. He replied that he had no quarrel with Britain and France. He would be prepared to hold a meeting to ensure peace. He waited for a reply and did not withdraw from Poland: war was inevitable.

The British nation was informed by radio that the Prime Minister would make an important announcement at 11 a.m. on 3 September. His message was clear. "As Germany has not complied with our demand that she withdraw her forces from Poland, a state of war now exists between Britain and France against Germany."

In Britain there was no cheering or waving of flags; the prospect of war had been hanging over the heads of the people for so long – everyone had hoped against hope that the war would never happen. Most people felt that

Chamberlain had done everything possible to prevent this catastrophe. The "peace at any price" brigade were of small number and of no consequence. The whole country viewed the prospect of being under the heel of Hitler and his gang as something they could never accept. They grimly accepted the dreaded consequences of the decision that had had to be made.

Joe Kennedy transmitted a long message to the President, giving all the information that the embassy had learned as to the strength of the German Army. The great unpreparedness of the British Forces, the appalling, inefficient, old-fashioned state of the French – there was no comparison between the two sides. The French seemed to think that all they had to do was to sit behind the Maginot Line defences and wait for the British and French Navies to starve out the Germans.

The feelings of the American people at home already showed that the US should stay out of the conflict. They remembered only too well the sacrifices made by their menfolk in the First World War. Despite pressure from the Jewish lobby in Washington, Roosevelt had to make his position clear. He made an official announcement to the world. The United States would remain neutral and would not be involved in the conflict.

"Why the hell they didn't sue for peace I don't know," Kennedy glared across the table at his son, Jack. "Thank goodness FDR has had the sense to take my advice. This announcement is just what the American people want, what they have been waiting for. You've been to Germany; you've already written about how well the country's run. Thank heaven there's no chance of Joe or yourself being called up, though with your back trouble I don't suppose there's any fear of them taking you."

Jack kept his mouth shut. It was best not to argue with his father. He had published his views of the practical problems in Europe – he had been highly critical. He had admired Germany, but now it seemed Hitler had gone too far; what sort of Europe would it be if Hitler won? What if Britain capitulated? How would America fare in such a new world? Had he been wrong all along? What was the alternative but to go to war? In the long run, how could America stay out of the conflict?

The subject of the First World War was something Joe did not talk about. He had managed to stay out of the army – he had made a packet.

On their return to Britain from the Continent, Rose and the family found a different kind of world. The round of social functions which had been part of Kathleen's life had disappeared. The whole country was being put on a war footing – windows being made ready to be blacked out, sandbags filled to protect doors and buildings, trenches being dug – waiting for the worst to happen. The world was falling apart. Bill was not around; she waited to hear where he had been posted. He had managed to get a 48-hour leave just before war was declared. They did not know when they would see each other again.

It was an open secret that the British Expeditionary Force, of which the Coldstream Guards unit to which Bill was attached was a part, would take up its position on the western flank of the Maginot Line defended by the French – that line of "impregnable" fortifications which the French had built to protect themselves against any possible invasion by Germany. Directly facing them was a similar line of fortifications built by the Germans – the Siegfried Line.

War had been declared, but on the land in Europe it was

stalemate – the two land forces remained facing each other across the no man's land between the two lines: the position did not change for months. Meanwhile, Poland had been divided in half by the two dictators – an uneasy peace.

Chamberlain's policy of appeasement having failed, he had now to form a cabinet to fight the war. He brought back Anthony Eden as Foreign Secretary and, best of all, the formidable Winston Churchill as Lord of the Admiralty.

The official statement made by Roosevelt was devastating news. How could Britain fight this war without help from the US? The blow was only slightly softened by unofficial – very unofficial and secret – news that America was considering how she could assist Britain. This was made through the contact in his embassy without Joe Kennedy's knowledge.

Although it was stalemate on land, the war at sea was being fought in deadly earnest. The German U-boats scored, to the great embarrassment of Britain, two outstanding successes: sinking the battleship *Ark Royal* by torpedoes while she was anchored in Scapa Flow, and then sinking an aircraft carrier by the same method.

The U-boat menace in the Atlantic soon made its presence felt, sinking numerous merchant ships which were bringing supplies to Britain. Was this a repeat of the 1914 war?

Kennedy's position was now becoming more and more untenable. He felt that the present lull would not last. How soon would it be before London suffered the same deluge of bombs that Warsaw had had to endure?

He decided that the family must go home, and during the winter they all returned to the States except for himself and his backward daughter, Rosemary. Rosemary had always been a great trial to the family. She was mentally retarded; she was presentable but had the mentality of a very young child. She had been placed in a special home for such cases in the countryside outside London. Joe, who hated that any of his children should be anything but perfect, heard that an operation could be performed which would greatly improve her mentally. Without saying anything to Rose, he arranged for a lobotomy to be performed; it was a disaster. Instead of improving her, it did just the opposite: she became virtually impossible to live with. So Joe sent her home, where she had to be placed in a special home for such unfortunate people.

At the embassy, although all matters were handled smoothly and efficiently, Joe was becoming aware that he was not getting involved with matters of importance. It seemed that Washington was in touch with the British Cabinet and that he was not being kept in the picture. He had not reported his conversation with the Irish Ambassador, O'Donnell, on the question of German U-boat bases in Ireland, and was suspicious to be told by him that somehow this demand had got to the ears of both the British and US Governments. Britain had instructed their ambassador in Dublin to seek an interview with De Valera. The message was simple: if Ireland agreed, there would be a state of war between Britain and Ireland. De Valera had to play for time. He informed the Germans that, in view of this, he could not agree to their demands.

This news, when received in Britain, was not unexpected. The U-boats had to have bases for them to operate in the Atlantic. Their decision of what to do had to be weighed against the news received from their Ambassador in Washington – the US would consider such a move as a breach of the neutrality agreed by Ireland and themselves.

Hitler decided to drop his demands; he would bring forward his next move – Norway.

Britain and France were now mobilising troops from their colonies abroad. Britain had support from Canada, Australia, India – all their colonies who had taken sides to support them. But the great problem in Britain was supplies; she would not be able to fight the war long-term without vast supplies of armaments – tanks, aircraft and ships. There was only one source capable of meeting her demands – America.

Britain's plight was brought home to Washington through their secret contacts. Roosevelt was in a dilemma; he had, by this time, realised that America would be faced with an impossible situation if Germany won. He had, however, promised the people of America that the US would be neutral. He found a compromise answer: he agreed to sell to Britain military equipment of all kinds on a cash-and-carry basis – all the equipment to be carried in British ships across the Atlantic.

The decision brought a howl of complaints from Germany. Hitler instructed his Ambassador to seek an interview with Roosevelt; he was to argue that, despite his policy of neutrality, Roosevelt was helping Britain to maintain their war effort, to the disadvantage of Germany – in fact, taking sides against Germany. This would surely sour relations between the two countries after Hitler had won the war. Roosevelt played down this complaint and let the agreement go ahead. The Press in America were in a quandary; they could see that, in the interest of the States, they should support Britain, but was this the first step in bringing America into the war? This they did not want at any price. But what would happen if Hitler conquered Europe?

15

The land stalemate throughout the winter of 1939 and spring of 1940 could not last. Hitler struck: his troops marched in and took over Denmark, and before the dust could settle, to the great dismay of Britain, he invaded Norway. The might of the German machine, and in particular the vast air power, made the defence of southern Norway impossible. Small German naval forces landed troops and took over the towns and parts of southern Norway.

Britain decided to make a stand by sending an expeditionary force to the area around the northern Norwegian port of Narvik. It was of no avail; although inflicting considerable damage to the German naval forces, Britain was forced to evacuate her troops, leaving the whole of the Norway coastline in the hands of the Germans – giving their U-boats and ships bases from which they could operate into the Atlantic. They now had no need for bases in Ireland.

14 May – the end of the stalemate – was the start of the blitzkrieg. Without warning, Hitler struck. The Germans attacked the Allies along the whole of the western front. They poured into Belgium, circumvented the northern end of the Maginot Line, swung south around the end of the Maginot Line, turned the whole of the French Army,

who retreated in complete disarray: they offered virtually no opposition. The Belgian and British forces tried to hold the line, but they were forced back – the British into an area of north-west France. Meanwhile, the Belgians tried to protect their homeland. They fought gallantly against impossible odds and before capitulating gave the British Army time to retreat to around the beaches of Dunkirk. The German armed forces seemed to be invincible.

In the light of this defeat, Chamberlain called on Parliament to form a national government of all political parties. Chamberlain, who was ill, had lost the confidence of the nation – he had to go. The nation called for one man, Winston Churchill, who was made Prime Minister. His deputy, the Labour Party leader, Clement Atlee, supported him loyally throughout the war.

Churchill addressed the nation over the radio: "I can promise you nothing but blood, sweat and tears. We will fight them on the beaches, in the towns, on the land – we will never surrender."

The plight of the British Army seemed hopeless. Hitler waited for them to surrender: why he did not press home his advantage will never be known. Had he run out of fuel or supplies? Whatever the reason, his forces were held by the thin ring of British defences around the encircled British Army with its back to the sea. Then – the miracle of Dunkirk. From the ports of the south and east coasts of Britain, hundreds of ships of all shapes and sizes – fishing boats, pleasure boats, privately owned yachts - set out across the Channel. The navy, with every ship it had in the vicinity, marshalled them to the beaches. The troops, with perfect discipline, moved onto the beaches and waded in to be hauled aboard and brought back to Britain, all this whilst being bombed and strafed by the Nazi Air Force. All the troops on the beaches were evacuated – over 330,000 troops – but not without the loss of many ships and men.

Had Hitler succeed in destroying or capturing the British forces at Dunkirk, then Britain would have been deprived of virtually the whole of their trained fighting forces at home. The troops had had to abandon all their heavy equipment – tanks, armoured vehicles, guns – everything

The French Army was overwhelmed. The Maginot Line had offered no real defence against the mobile might of the Germans. They had no modern tanks to withstand the onslaught.

Behind it all, it seemed from the outset that it was true that the French parliament had no stomach for the fight. The situation was chaotic. The army had no reply – in a matter of days Pierre Laval sued for peace. He bent over backwards to cooperate with all Hitler's demands: the price paid – Paris was never bombed. Hitler, with all the Nazi bands playing, his triumphant, highly polished troops in perfect order, marched in and took over the city.

Britain, standing alone, awaited the onslaught.

16

Joe Kennedy had very mixed feelings when he heard of the cash-and-carry arrangement which had been made behind his back. He was becoming aware of the vast quantity of supplies that were involved, and soon came to the conclusion that, although Britain had started the war with very great reserves of foreign assets, as they had to be sold to pay for the supplies, they would be exhausted in no time. What would be the situation then?

Immediately after Dunkirk, he had heard that Hitler was, behind the scenes, making overtures to Britain to negotiate peace. This, to Joe, seemed the only sensible course to take. Britain, he felt, could not possibly survive. His relationship with the Churchill-led Parliament was becoming strained – and behind a veneer of friendship, he knew that he was becoming more and more unpopular with them, and also with the British Press.

At home, Joe Junior had returned to Harvard and was getting involved with local politics in pursuit of a political career. In support of his father, he had formed a society at Harvard specifically to demand that there should be no American intervention in Europe. At the same time, Jack's book on the flabbiness of democracy in Europe, which had been backed with Joe's money, was having a very mixed reception.

There was, however, great news for Kick; she had heard that Bill was safe. He had been evacuated with his unit from the port of Boulogne at the time of Dunkirk, just before the Germans moved in and took the town.

Of all the Kennedy family, Kick was the only one to stand up to her father. A meeting of the family erupted into a terrific row. Kick turned on her father. 'You made me come home when I wanted to stay in Britain – you have done everything you can to prevent America supporting them. You say that you have saved America from being in the war – well, what now? Britain is standing alone – what do you want? Britain to be taken over by the Nazis? If they were, where would you stand? Would America allow Hitler to rule the whole of Europe, allow him to slaughter all the Jews in Europe? The only hope for Britain to survive is for us to pour in all the military equipment, aircraft, ships we can. We are their only hope. They will fight for their country to the bitter end. I wish I were there.'

Joe was livid. 'Don't you dare talk to me like that, girl. I know what is best for our country. I am looking after all our interests. I will not be insulted by my own daughter.'

He stormed out, Kick standing alone in tears as the family left the room. As Joe Junior left, he whispered into her ear, 'Well done, Kick.'

The weather in the summer of 1940 was beautiful. Hitler struck. Hermann Goering, Chief of the German Air Force, sent over Britain swarms of fighters escorting bombers to eliminate Britain's airfields. The fighters of the RAF, mainly Spitfires and manned, in the main, by young, recently trained pilots, took off to meet them. The whole country held its breath while the greatest air battle of all times took place – the Battle of Britain. The air fleets were locked in deadly embrace. With skill and daring, the young RAF pilots fought without respite and at great loss to themselves. Goering poured in more fighters, but the RAF shot them down. The bombers that did get through were hunted and destroyed. The German wastage rate was too great – they had to give up. The RAF fighter units, although badly depleted, were intact. The British airfields were intact. The Battle of Britain had been won – the impossible had been achieved. Hitler had no alternative: he had to abandon his plan to invade Britain. Churchill spoke to the nation on the radio, paying tribute to the fighter pilots of the RAF: "Never in the field of human conflict was so much owed by so many to so few."

Joe reported to Washington – he made a speech which caused great concern in America and resentment in Britain.

He said, "The news that the RAF have succeeded in containing the German Air Force and for the present prevented a Nazi invasion of Britain is a great tribute to the gallantry of those young pilots. But this does not affect the overall pattern of the conflict; the strength of the German military forces will gradually wear down the ability of Britain to resist. To keep up this defence they must obtain vast supplies of military equipment of all kinds – and they will bring all the pressure they can on America to supply them. This we must not do – we must remain strictly neutral. I am sure that the great majority of our people agree with me. Our government should continue to maintain this stand. Hitler is aware of our position and in order that this terrible conflict be brought to an end Britain should sue for peace."

This speech caused such resentment in Britain that Roosevelt made a statement to the effect that the views that he had expressed were not the official views of the US Government. Joe was livid.

Following his defeat in the air, Hitler wasted no time. He started the massive night bombing of London and the industrial cities of Britain. The effect was devastating, both in the great number of casualties and the untold damage caused. There was little defence in the light of the number of bombers involved. This was something the people of Britain had to endure virtually to the end of the war – Hitler's plan to bomb Britain into submission.

17

Joe Kennedy had had enough. He did not care for the nightly bombing, getting away from London into the country whenever he could. He felt that he had been snubbed: he knew that he was unpopular. He was still the blue-eyed boy of the Irish, but that counted for nought in the present situation.

Joe sent a message to Washington, "I should like to speak to the President as soon as possible; it is most important." It seemed a long time until the phone rang.

"Hello Joe – hope you're well," said FDR's familiar voice on the phone.

"Fine thanks, Mr President. Hope you're the same."

"I'm OK, Joe. What can I do for you?"

"Well, Mr President, as you know I am strongly dedicated to the cause of peace. I know that unless Britain agrees to make peace with Hitler, which I am sure he wants, then I think war is inevitable. I made my views strongly heard, as well as to insist that America would give no support to either side in the event of war and would remain strictly neutral. My face does not fit, Mr President. I want out – I want to be relieved of the job."

FDR replied, "Joe, I am very sorry that things have not worked out as I had hoped. I thought you were just the right person for such an important post. We have been friends for so many years, Joe. I would not wish you to carry on now that I know how you feel. I will see that arrangements are made for you to be replaced straight away. I think that you have done very well in very difficult circumstances. Best wishes to yourself and Rose. Goodbye."

Joe put down the phone. You two-faced bastard, he thought.

Before he left for home, Joe visited Chamberlain to say farewell.

"Mr Chamberlain, as you have probably heard, I am going back to America, but before I left for home I felt that I should come and wish you goodbye – and give you my best wishes."

Chamberlain replied, "Mr Kennedy, thank you very much for coming to see me, I do appreciate it." Sitting in his chair with a blanket over his knees he looked a frail and sad figure. He was dying of cancer. He continued, "It is fair to say that, although we both have very different views of how the present world situation should be resolved, we both have one main concern: what is best for our nation. I have reached the end of the road and have handed over my responsibilities. I would not wish on you or anyone the decisions I have had to make on behalf of my country. I tried so hard to follow your ideas that we should keep the peace by all means. I even went to meet Hitler and obtained a signed agreement from him that he had no more military ambitions in Europe. I came home, was cheered to the echo – Peace in our time. But of course, Mr Kennedy, he had no intention of keeping his word and I was then criticised for what I had agreed. I would not wish on anyone what I had to do when I had to tell the nation we were at war – what suffering, hardship and even death, to many of those who were listening to me on the radio that dreadful day, would follow. Thank you again for coming to say goodbye. I shall not live to see the end of this carnage – who knows where it will all end and whether you will have to change your views should your country be threatened. Goodbye."

* * *

"Here's to us, we brought it off." It was a very private celebration party at Charles Ruston's flat – just the four of them. Ruston, Smithers and their wives. They drank the toast in champagne.

"I'm glad it's all over, aren't you, George?" he said. "I never thought we would be able to keep the whole set up secret and that no one in your Embassy or at our Foreign Office would suspect what we were doing. I was called in to see Halifax this morning. He had just heard that Joe was being replaced. He said that the PM and the Cabinet were delighted. He said that the private arrangement we had had now served its purpose and that all matters between the States and ourselves would revert to normal channels. He said that the PM was very pleased at the way we had handled this very delicate situation and asked me to give you his thanks."

"I had a similar message from Cordell Hull," said Smithers. "FDR dreamt up the whole scheme – it worked, we managed to keep Joe Kennedy in the dark and now he is going back to Washington. I can appreciate how the British Government feel about that. Well, thank goodness this cloak and dagger business is finished and we can get back to our normal jobs."

They finished off the champagne.

Shortly after they returned to the States, Joe and Rose were invited by Roosevelt to dinner. As it was a social occasion, he had also invited Eleanor to be there. She accepted reluctantly – she did not care for the Kennedys. The marriage between FDR and Eleanor was nothing but a façade. They had not had any proper relations as man and wife for many years. However, she was a powerful influence in the Democratic Party, performing official duties and supporting the Party in every way.

The dinner party was not a success. After an enthusiastic welcome FDR said, "Well, Joe, I expect that you are pleased to be back with the family. I feel that life in London is not at all pleasant – the bombing is terrible."

"Yes," said Joe, "I sure am glad to be home. From the outset I knew that I should not have taken on the job and frankly, knowing my views I feel that you should not have pressed me to accept it. I feel that I should have served my country by being in the Administration here. In London my position was untenable – everyone to my face was polite and friendly but behind my back they turned up their noses at me. They hated my support for a United Ireland."

It irked FDR that he had to stand for the way Kennedy spoke to him, but he had to take it. He could not split with him and let him swing to the other side. The election for his third term was not far ahead; he knew that he was losing some support in the country. He had to rely on Joe and John Fitzgerald to see that he was supported by the Irish-American voters whom they controlled. Those votes could swing the result; he had to keep in with Joe. He succeeded in soft-soaping him; they parted on, apparently, friendly terms. Joe was still angry, but he had decided that he would stay loyal to the Democrats – after all, he had to think of Joe Junior's future. One day, if he had anything to do with it, Joe Junior would be sitting in Roosevelt's chair.

18

Joe was right about one thing: Mussolini had been sitting on the fence. With the defeat of the Allies on the Continent, he thought Hitler was invincible; he jumped on the bandwagon and declared war on the Allies. This, of course, extended the theatre of war into the whole of the Middle East and North Africa.

He immediately got a bloody nose; his large army, based in his North African colony, Libya, marched on Egypt to meet the British forces based on the border to protect that country. Although vastly outnumbered, the British attached and decimated them. They were forced to retreat until finally making a stand at Tobruk.

The British took literally thousands of POWs, who remained in camps in the desert for the rest of the war.

The Italians had built up a modern fleet. They had six battleships, beautifully designed, as fast as any at sea, but not heavily armour-protected. On 11 November 1940 they were tucked neatly at anchor in the outer harbour of Taranto at the foot of Italy, the whole area heavily protected by anti-aircraft guns and balloons. From the British aircraft carrier *Illustrious,* twenty-one Swordfish bombers and torpedo bombers took off to attack them. The old-fashioned, slow planes seemed almost like relics of the last war. They flew through a gap in the balloon screen and delivered their missiles. They sank three of the battleships and put a fourth out of action. The Italian Navy had been reduced to two battleships for the loss of two Swordfish bombers. The Italians were stunned.

By this time, Britain was being freely supplied by America with every kind of military, naval and air force equipment but, as Joe Kennedy has predicted, foreign financial reserves were running out – she could no longer pay. The solution – on 12 March 1941, whilst officially declaring her policy of neutrality, a bill was passed in the Senate that these supplies would be provided on a "lend-lease" basis; in other words, Britain had unlimited credit.

Hitler was beside himself when he heard the news. He had assumed that when the cash-and-carry agreement came to an end as British funds were exhausted, the supplies would dry up; now it seemed that, under the new agreement, America was prepared to supply unlimited arms and equipment. He instructed his Ambassador in Washington to make the strongest possible protest – this was clearly a complete breach of neutrality. He demanded that the lend-lease act be rescinded; Roosevelt ignored the demand.

Kennedy viewed this development with great concern; he had been so sure all along that Britain was finished, but this would strengthen her hand. On every occasion, whenever he could, he argued the case that America must stay out of the war. He was, however, delighted that the Irish Premier, De Valera, who had been walking a tightrope, had been able to keep Ireland out of the war – Churchill would dearly have liked to have sea bases on the west coast of Ireland. His relations with De Valera were, to say the least, not cordial.

De Valera's only hope of staying out of the conflict was

by playing the America card. The American-Irish were mainly anti-British and could bring pressure on the US Government to prevent Britain making any demands on Ireland and, at the same time, make it impossible for Hitler to take any action against Ireland.

Hitler was carrying out his threat – trying to bomb Britain into submission. On the black night of 18 April it was estimated that no less than 450 bombers rained down their tons of explosives and incendiaries on the capital – London burned.

By June, America was being driven closer and closer to the brink of war. Ships carrying supplies to Britain were being sunk in such numbers that something had to be done. The U-boats, particularly off the shores of the east coast of America, were virtually free from attack by air and by the British Navy. The merchant ships in the area were at their mercy.

Roosevelt spoke to the nation; he had instructed the US Navy command that their patrols were to protect Allied shipping in the western approaches. This had a profound effect on American public opinion. Was this the first stage of America being forced into the conflict? The Germans accused America of taking warlike actions against them. The U-boat commanders were in an invidious position; American patrols could hunt them down, but if they retaliated and sank a US vessel, that would be tantamount to war.

19

Joe Kennedy, on his return to the States, settled down spending most of his time either at home or at his other home at Palm Springs. He waited to hear from FDR, hoping some senior post connected with the government, but none was forthcoming. He still retained his flat in Washington, which he used occasionally, and one day received a phone call. His caller asked if he could visit him at the flat on a matter of importance. The caller was Colonel Charles Lindbergh. Joe agreed.

Charles Lindbergh was an international hero: he had a few years earlier been the first man to fly the Atlantic solo in a single-engined airplane. His plane, *The Spirit of St Louis,* had left the west coast and had touched down – his fuel virtually exhausted – a few miles west of Paris. He was universally acclaimed. Following his success, he visited the main countries in Europe, where he was mobbed. He was particularly acclaimed in Germany, where he was proudly shown all the achievements of the Nazi regime; how Germany was now a well-disciplined industrial nation of great military might. He was greatly impressed. Although disagreeably surprised at their invasions of Czechoslovakia and Poland, he did not think for one moment that Britain would, in the long term, be able to stand out against Germany.

"Is that Mr Kennedy?"

Joe spoke into the phone, "Yes".

"This is Charles Lindbergh – I am very pleased to be able to speak with you – I hope you are well."

"Fine thanks," said Joe.

"I am ringing to ask you to become an active member and supporter of our American First Committee. I am sure that with your views, which are identical to mine and those of the committee's, that if you joined us it would add greatly to the considerable pressure that we are bringing on the government – to ensure that under no circumstances is America to allow itself to become embroiled in this conflict. Our movement is gaining terrific momentum throughout the country – our people do not want their sons to be sent off to be killed in some distant country in a bloody conflict which should never have been started. Can I take it that you will join us – your name will give even more strength to our campaign?"

Joe was in a quandary, of course he agreed with the committee's purposes – but if things went the other way where would he stand? He would be out on a limb. As Chamberlain had said – who knows how this would end? He could not risk sticking his neck out.

"I am very honoured that you should ask me to join your committee but I shall have to consider the matter. I feel that I could probably be more effective as I am at present – quietly lobbying for peace rather than appearing to force the issue. I will phone you if I decide to join you."

"I am sorry you cannot agree immediately. I look forward to hearing from you. Goodbye," said Lindbergh.

Following his re-election for a second term in 1936, FDR had promised the nation that the country's armed forces would be built up to ensure the safety of the nation. A large naval construction programme was under way. Roosevelt had every reason to be pleased that these plans were bearing fruit. The US Government, in the light of current events, without appearing to overplay its hand, started a national drive to build up the Reserve Forces. Joe Junior was coming to the conclusion that, despite their wishes, the country was being pushed nearer and nearer to war. He joined the American Air Force Reserve to be trained as a pilot. Joe Senior was livid.

"Why the hell have you done it? Just because the government have urged the youth of the country that it is their patriotic duty to volunteer to join the Reserves? Is that the reason? You know damn well that Britain is finished – you've agreed with me on that – and now you tell me that you have joined the American Air Force Reserve to become a pilot."

"I did Pa", said Joe Junior, "but I no longer agree with you – events have overtaken us. If Britain is finished, as you say, where does that leave us? That madman Hitler rampaging and jack-booting across the whole of Europe, everyone subservient to the so-called German master race. Britain is the only bulwark against this; if she falls then we shall have to be sufficiently strong to be able to maintain our position. I don't know when or how this will all end, whether we shall be drawn into a war or not – that's why I have joined the Reserve – and until then we must get to Britain all the military equipment and planes that we possibly can."

Joe did not answer – he was having to face facts which he did not like.

Jack was not to be outdone; he applied to join the US Navy. His health record was against him but, being a Kennedy, he was accepted, albeit only fit for non-combat duties.

"Joe told me two or three days ago that he had joined the US Air Force Reserve and that he had discussed it with you;" Jack said to his father.

"Discussed it with me!" Joe said. "He told me what he had done. Had I known beforehand I would certainly have done all I could to stop him. It is absurd that in view of our position and views he should have done so."

"Well Pa," said Jack, "I think you should know that I have joined the US Navy Reserve." Joe was shocked, "This is ridiculous," he said, "you cannot be classed as A1 fit – they will not take you."

"But they have. I used our name and pulled a few strings – at the moment for non-combat duties – but I'll work on that."

"How can you?" said Joe. "You went to Germany, came back and told everyone what a wonderful job Hitler is doing in running the country, how he has made Germany such a great nation. You published a book citing all these views and I had to get the damn thing withdrawn at a hell of a cost – what do you say to that?"

"I say how much I resent being hoodwinked and taken for a sucker by those bastards," said Jack. "I have discussed the whole situation at length with Joe – and now I am in entire agreement with the views which I understand he has expressed to you." Joe had no answer.

To make matters worse, Kathleen was pestering him to death.

"I've had another letter from Bill," she said. "He says that with the conscripts his unit is gradually being built up." She turned to her father. "I hear that both Joe and John have joined the Reserves – that is what I should have done if I had been a man. You know I want to get back to London, Father, why can't you get me a job in the Embassy there?"

"Go back to London – all that bombing, black-out restrictions – despite all that you want to go back to see that Lord Hartington you are always on about? You know very well that there's no future in that. But as far as going back to London – you are not going back." Kathleen looked at her mother and shrugged her shoulders. One day she'd get back.

In an attempt to placate her, using his contacts and pulling strings, he got her a job as a reporter on the *Times Herald* in Washington. The job brought her into contact with the main political and other important figures of the day – after all, she *was* a Kennedy. She enjoyed the job, but she still wanted to get back to Britain.

To make life difficult for Joe and Rose, Jack, who had been given a desk job at navy HQ in Washington, became heavily involved with a girl named Inga. Jack was always getting involved with some girl or other, but this was different. The Press got hold of the affair and started to make enquiries into her background. They found out that she was German, that her family were associated with the National Socialist Party – the Nazis; that she had met Hitler. The Press had a field day – it hit the headlines.

"How the devil do you explain this?" Joe slammed the paper down for Jack to see the headlines: "John F. Kennedy Nazi Girlfriend".

"It's just not true," said Jack. "The whole thing is a pack of lies. Inga's grandparents were German, but how many Americans have German ancestor? She has no political connections with Germany , she is as much American as we are."

"That's not what it says here – her family are associated with the National Socialist Party – the Nazis – it even says that with her family, she had a meeting with Hitler."

"It is a damn disgrace that papers can get away with lies like this," said Jack.

"There's one thing," said Joe, "you are to stop seeing her – whether it is true or not I cannot have any member of the family being associated with this sort of scandal. What the hell do you think it will do to our reputation?"

"I don't see why I should stop seeing her," said Jack. "I'll try and find out if there is anything behind this allegation."

The following day Jack succeeded in getting an interview with J. Edgar Hoover, Chief of the FBI.

"Thank you for seeing me at short notice, Mr Hoover," he said. "A great friend of mine is being vilified quite unjustly by the Press, who, without any proof or justification, are printing that she is associated with the Nazis. Knowing that your excellent organisation has knowledge of all those who are suspected of being enemies of the US, I am taking the liberty of asking you if you would confirm that these accusations are quite untrue, so that I can have these lies repudiated."

Edgar Hoover took a time to reply. He said, "Mr Kennedy, it is the duty of the FBI to protect the interests of the State. I have had details of your problem brought before me – if there is any truth in the allegations you will appreciate that I would not be in a position to discuss them with you. On the other hand, if there is no evidence of truth in the allegations, again I could not advise you because if at a later date the issue had to be looked at again I would have placed the FBI in an invidious position – and this I am not prepared to do. I am pleased to have met you, Mr Kennedy. I am sorry I cannot help you. Goodbye."

The Navy Board, however, took a very poor view of the matter. They transferred Jack out of Washington to an operational naval base in Connecticut. On the quiet, Jack still maintained contact with Inga, until finally Joe did manage to put a stop to it.

If this was not enough, Joe Junior started to escort a girl who, Rose learned, was a Protestant. Once more there was a Kennedy family row.

It seemed incongruous that Rose, who was fully aware of her husband's infidelities, should turn a blind eye to them and yet hold the family strictly to the rigid demands of the Roman Catholic Church. The possibility of a Kennedy marrying outside the Church was quite unthinkable and could not possibly be countenanced. Fortunately for Rose, that affair petered out.

20

On 22 June the war in Europe took a most dramatic and unexpected turn: Germany declared war on Russia. So much for the signed non-aggression pact; so much for Hitler's word – it was now obvious that this had been part of Hitler's plan from the start. Had he been able to make Britain sue for peace, he would have had a completely free hand to conquer all lands from the North Sea to the Urals. Even so, he went ahead with this, his greatest gamble. The vast forces which he had stationed in the west to participate in the invasion of Britain were now turned and thrown against the Russians.

The Russians reeled against the onslaught. They had no defence against the initial mechanised advance. Hitler's armies advanced north towards the outskirts of Leningrad, towards Moscow and advanced at speed due east. Churchill acted quickly: he sent Anthony Eden to Moscow. The thought of being in partnership with Russia nauseated him, but this was a case of survival. Eden signed with Stalin an Anglo-Russian military alliance against Germany.

Churchill had no illusions; this was a pact to ensure the defeat of Hitler. He had no faith in Stalin's word – he hated Communism.

The news from Russia was not good – the Germans laid

siege to Moscow and Leningrad and were driving ever eastwards.

The question of whether America would be involved in the conflict was resolved in a way that could never have been foreseen or even imagined. On 8 December 1941, without warning, Japanese bombers flying from carriers protected by battleships and destroyers rained down innumerable bombs on the American Pacific fleet moored peacefully at anchor in its base in Pearl Harbor.

The Emperor of Japan, in a rare radio message to his nation, stated that Japan had declared war on America and Britain. All Japanese, military and civilian, must be prepared to lay down their lives for the glory of the nation.

Churchill flew to Washington, the first of many talks with Roosevelt to prepare the joint actions and strategy they would take to defeat their common enemies.

21

The year of 1942 was a year of defeats and despair. The Japanese made sweeping victories throughout the whole of the Pacific, Hitler continued his relentless drive against the Russians.

The might of the German Army was such that Hitler was able to send troops, tanks and equipment to bolster up the Italians in North Africa, with a view once more to attacking Egypt.

At home, Joe was still champing at the bit at not being involved with the war effort. He and Rose were mad with Joe Junior; after completing his training and becoming a fully qualified pilot he had volunteered to be transferred to the American unit of the RAF. To Joe's great concern, he was posted to Britain and there he spent most of his time on Lancaster bombers. His squadron in Britain was largely engaged in patrolling the eastern approaches of the Atlantic to protect shipping and tracking submarines.

Jack Kennedy had at last got the sort of posting he had wanted. All his life he had suffered from ill health and back trouble, never being able to keep up with the sporting activities of his brothers. Now he could prove himself, prove he was no also-ran. He had been posted to the Pacific, in command of one of a small squadron of torpedo boats on a small island. Their job was to attack

Japanese shipping, whether naval vessels, troop carriers or convoys. His instructions were simple: when they had news of an approaching convoy, which intelligence had reported had an escort of destroyers, he, together with other similar craft, left base in the middle of the night to take up different positions in the path of the convoy, then cut engines and wait. As soon as dawn appeared and they were able to see the dark shapes of the approaching vessels they were each to choose their own target, open up full speed towards it, fire their torpedoes, and get the hell back to base. Just as Jack was about to give the order a Jap destroyer came out of the darkness at full speed – obviously they had been spotted. The destroyer smashed into them and the crew of six were able to do just one thing – jump overboard. As dawn broke the crew were all swimming around or hanging on to pieces of timber or anything that floated – all that was left of their boat which had been smashed into smithereens. They swam to form a group. They had only one casualty. There was no sign of the destroyer, it had disappeared into the dawn, not a sign of any shipping, the sea was deserted. One of the crew shouted, "Look – land!" They all turned and approximately two miles away there was indeed land. Jack shouted his orders, "We all stick together to swim ashore. Johnson here has a hell of a smashed knee – find some floating timber and secure him to it. Collect together any suitable floating debris for us to tow and to hang on to if we tire – the strongest swimmers help the others. We stay together – no one goes off on their own – we stay together and we arrive together." They did. They staggered ashore a deserted tree-lined beach. They helped Johnson, laying him in the shade of a tree on the perimeter of the beach, and looked around them.

"What sort of place is this?" said one of the crew. "Looks like a South Sea island picture post card."

"I think that's just what it is," said Jack.

"We'll soon find out." He said he would stay with Johnson; two of the crew to explore to left and two to the right – and report back in an hour. In less than an hour he was surprised when the four of them came through the trees towards him.

"This is a ruddy South Sea island all right," said one of them. "It's about the size of a ruddy football pitch – not a blooming thing on it except trees and palm trees. Not a hula-hula girl in sight," brought a laugh.

Other than a few coconuts, there was no food or water on the island – they had to get away. When they had arrived on the island there had been a heat haze – this had now lifted and they saw to their delight another island only a mile or so away. They spent a miserable night on the beach, but next day they managed to swim across to the other island. As they rested on the beach one of the party was sent out to explore. He had only been gone a short time when they saw him in the distance waving his shirt frantically, and heard him shouting at the top of his voice. A US patrol boat had appeared around the headland, sent out to see if there was any trace of them. They had spotted him, and in no time they were picked up and safely aboard the patrol boat.

Jack came home as a hero – Joe saw to that. He got the incident the greatest possible publicity – the way he had virtually been able to save the lives of his crew, and Jack got a medal. The navy however took a different view as to how Jack should have acted prior to his boat being sighted and sunk by the destroyer. This was Jack's one and only active combat involvement – after this incident, perhaps because of it, he was laid up with back troubles and on recovery was posted to a non-combat home-based unit.

"Why the hell doesn't he stay on the ground – and why the hell doesn't he get posted to an American unit? Then I could get him sent back here." Joe had heard that Joe Junior had completed his tour of flying duty; he was entitled to ask to be grounded. Joe did not know, but it was not quite so simple as that. Joe Junior had come through safely, but many of his colleagues had not.

But the real reason he wanted to stay in England was very different: he had fallen in love with a girl named Mary Weston, the wife of a British officer who was serving in the Middle East. Her marriage, in the autumn of 1939, was only one month old before her husband had been posted abroad. She had not, of course, seen him since and the letters between them had become stilted and strained. She was madly in love with Joe. They had agreed that as soon as the war was over she would seek a divorce and that they would get married.

Joe Junior had played the field, but this was for real. Being a Roman Catholic and seeking to marry a divorced woman would bring problems that, at this point in time, he did not wish to contemplate. After seeing death at such close quarters, his religious convictions were wearing a little thin. He had learned of an experimental unit which was being formed. Highly secret, it was in its initial stages and would not become operational for some time. He volunteered; it solved his problem – he was able to rent a cottage in a village in Essex, not far from the airfield where the unit had been located. He was able to be with Mary whenever he was not on duty. He knew from the outset that the project was highly dangerous.

22

The face of Europe was changing. Under the initial terms of the French surrender, the Germans had agreed that only approximately half of that country would be occupied but, with the co-operation of the traitor Laval, the Germans, as usual, broke the agreement and their troops took over and occupied the whole of France.

The operations in the field in Egypt were in the hands of General Bernard Montgomery.

He launched a terrific attack on Rommel against his prepared defences at El Alamein.

Rommel's defences collapsed. He rapidly retreated back across the desert to Tobruk to hold the line for a time. Four German and eight Italian divisions were captured. This was a great victory.

In the Far East, the Japanese were also trying to consolidate their gains. This war was mainly a sea war. The Japanese had been preparing for the war for years. They had the most formidable fleet of battleships, carriers, cruisers and destroyers, together with all the supporting craft – they had numerous submarines. They had realised the power of bombers against surface ships and built up a carrier borne fleet of bombers and supporting fighters.

Their early and easy success in sinking the great battleships of the Royal Navy, the *Repulse* and the *Hood*, weakened Britain's power in that area of the war. The American Navy also suffered greatly against this overwhelming superiority of power. The initial losses suffered at Pearl Harbour were soon made up. The country was now geared to make all weapons of war at an unprecedented speed.

In Britain, the position was serious, if not desperate. The German U-boats, operating from Norway, Germany and the north-west havens on the coast of France, were wreaking havoc with supplies destined for Britain across the Atlantic. Then – survival: a team of British scientists perfected a radar device which enabled ships or aircraft to pinpoint the position of U-boats wherever they were.

The effect was dramatic – the success rate in destroying submarines soared. The Germans waited anxiously for their U-boats to return to base: many did not. Within two months of the fitting of the equipment generally the U-boats were doomed. They were still a menace but could now be easily controlled. Admiral Doenitz, head of the German Navy, reported to the German High Command that the one weapon which would have brought Britain to her knees had been neutralised.

23

The love affair between Bill Hartington and Kick had blossomed. Although they had not seen each other for over two years, their letters were frequent and endearing.

Kick had made up her mind that, despite all the obstacles that would be put in her way, she was going to marry Hartington. She kept her decision to herself; she knew that her parents would do everything in their power to stop her. The standing that Joe and Rose had in the Roman Catholic Church was such that, as far as they were concerned, they could not allow any of their children to marry outside their faith.

Come what may, Kick was going to be Lady Hartington and, one day, Duchess of Devonshire. She plagued her parents constantly. She wanted to get back to Britain. They would not agree. Why should she risk going back to Britain to face all the restrictions, the austerity and, above all, the bombing? She managed it.

* * *

Kick was beside herself with joy. She burst in on her mother and father, "They have accepted me", she said, waving the document she had received. "I'm going to London".

"Whatever do you mean?" asked Rose. "What have you done? Who have accepted you?"

"The American Red Cross – they are having to set up a large organisation to look after the personnel problems, the welfare and the entertainment for all the vast number of American Forces personnel who are being sent to Britain. So I made enquiries as to who was running the show – pulled a few strings. This has just arrived: they have accepted me. I am to report to the main recruitment centre here and I shall then be transported to London. It's just what I wanted and even better – I am to work at the main centre in the West End."

"It's damned ridiculous," said Joe, "we've been through all this before. You say you don't care about the danger – the bombing restrictions, the blackout. I've managed to get you a job as a political reporter here in Washington, where you would have the making of a great career, and you have thrown it all up to join the American Red Cross. Don't you think we know what's behind all this? You're not doing it from any sense of patriotic duty – anything to get back to Hartington. You are damned obsessed with the fellow."

Rose interposed, "I can well understand how you feel, dear, but you must be sensible. You must realise that there is no future in this relationship, in view of all the religious differences, the different social positions, there is no likelihood of your marrying him. Anyway, has he given you any hint that he wants to marry you?"

"Of course your mother is right," said Joe. "You are giving up everything you have here for just a pipe dream. What sort of work will you do in London – serve in the forces canteen?"

"I don't know exactly what I shall be doing when I get to London – but whatever I do it will be helping towards the final defeat of my country's enemies. Yes, it is true that I want to be near Bill – I love him and I know that he loves me. That's as far as I can see at present. And you sneer at the work I shall be doing in London, helping our troops with their domestic problems, helping to entertain them – yes, even helping in the canteen. I told you before if I were a man I would be in the fighting services – I'm proud of Joe and Jack for joining up. Are you proud, Father? Proud of the way you tried to belittle Britain, proud of trying to stop all the supplies they needed, proud of being prepared for Hitler to take over the whole of Europe as long as you could keep the USA from being involved? What of Pearl Harbor? What are your views now?"

As Kick left the room she made one parting shot, "I have signed all the documents, I am committed. I am over twenty-one – I shall be going to Britain."

Rose turned to Joe, but he made no reply. Everything he had worked for for years was in ruins. He had been proven wrong – he was at loggerheads with his children. What should he do? He must make a U-turn, he must get back into the mainstream, his efforts must be to support the States and their allies to win this war.

Rose sighed. She had always supported Joe against her better judgement in the past, now at last she was able to openly support the war effort. She smiled to herself. She liked Bill Hartington in spite of everything. Could it be possible that one day they would marry? Could she one day be the grandmother to a future Duke of Devonshire?

Throughout the centuries, the house of Devonshire had always been in the forefront of British politics. During the previous 150 years a Devonshire, or a nominee of the Devonshires, had always held the Conservative seat of West Derbyshire. Towards the end of 1943 the MP who was currently holding the seat (a distant relation of the family) decided that he would retire. This was either arranged or a fortunate coincidence as far as Bill was concerned. It was too good an opportunity to be missed. Bill decided that he would prefer to be an MP, rather than stay in the army. He put himself forward to the local Conservative Association to be considered as their candidate for the forthcoming by-election, subject to him being released from the army. Being a Devonshire, he was of course selected. He applied to the army to grant him his release and again, being who he was, this was granted. He was placed in the army reserve to be called up if required.

* * *

Kick was thrilled with the news: they would be able to be together he was out of the services. She was no stranger to the thrill of electioneering in her home town with the family, but electioneering in the countryside in Derbyshire was very different. She loved it: she attended all his meetings, met the farmers and their wives, partook in the canvassing and all the hundred and one jobs involved. The lady voters were all for meeting her. Fancy – an American – daughter of a millionaire. Was she going to marry Lord Hartington?

She had, since her return, once more become very friendly with Lady Astor. At the outbreak of war the Cliveden Set had made a hasty retreat. No longer could they argue for appeasement; they were now all loyal supporters of the government against that bloody man, Hitler.

Prior to the long build-up to the election, Bill and Kick were invited by Lady Astor to visit her at her house in her constituency in Plymouth. They decided to spend a holiday in the West Country. They were appalled to see the damage caused by the German bombing of the centre of

Plymouth itself – it had been gutted. The German bombers had also badly damaged the nearby naval dockyard, Davenport. Between them, Bill and Kick had scrounged, borrowed and, by pooling their own petrol coupons to get enough fuel, used Bill's small sports car to tour the beautiful countryside of Devon.

On the last day of their holiday, on their way home, Bill branched off into the seaside town of Torquay and then onto the nearby fishing village of Brixham. They parked the car and made their way to the quayside.

"As you keep pestering me about the family history, I thought you would like to see this," he said. He pointed to a statue which had been erected at the head of a flight of steps leading down to the harbour water. She walked up to the statue and read the inscription: "At these steps William of Orange landed in England."

"Whoever was William of Orange, and what's it got to do with you?"

"It was he who made the fourth Earl of Devonshire the first Duke of Devonshire."

"All right, I want to know – tell me how."

"I'll tell you over lunch."

They made their way along the quay, across the cobbled road to the Fisherman's Arms. Sitting in the smoky room with a plate of fish and chips in front of them and a glass of local cider, as promised he continued his saga of the Devonshires.

"Like America, we had a civil war here – of course, well before yours. This was at the time of King Charles I. You see, he thought that he had the divine right to rule, so he refused to give the British Parliament any power at all; in fact, he dissolved Parliament and didn't recall it. This caused terrific dissent in the country, and two opposing sides were formed – the King's supporters, called Cavaliers, and the parliamentarians under their leader, Oliver Cromwell, called the Roundheads. Well, after many bloody battles the Roundheads won, accused Charles of treason, found him guilty, and had him beheaded. Then the country was a republic under Cromwell.

'Of course the Devonshires always supported the monarchy: we had a rough time. Some of the family had to flee to the Continent to save their lives. Virtually all our houses and land were confiscated. Well, Cromwell's Republican Government soon became very unpopular with the people; they didn't like the very strict regime. They had to comply with a very dour form of puritan Christianity, which denied them any type of pleasure, even dancing. The pressure became so great that Parliament had to concede, and to get the country back to normal they brought back Charles I's son to become King Charles II. This was great for us: we had all our wealth, houses and land restored to us. Because of our loyalty to the monarchy, we were once more back in the corridors of power. Charles agreed to be the head of the official Church of England. There was still a certain amount of animosity between the Protestants and the Catholics, but Charles managed not to take sides.

"There was a problem: Charles had no legitimate son. His heir was his brother, James, Duke of York, who was an avid Roman Catholic, and when he came to the throne the friction between the two different religious faiths started all over again. The real issue was that, although Charles did not have a legitimate son, he had an illegitimate son, whom he had made the Duke of Monmouth.

"During Charles' reign, there was terrific friction between the Duke of York and the Duke of Monmouth. As

James was Roman Catholic and Monmouth Church of England, public opinion was largely in favour of Monmouth. He tried to persuade the King to make him legitimate and therefore heir to the throne, but Charles would not face up to the issue, and so his brother James came to the throne. Monmouth, who was very popular in the West Country, raised an army to march on London, but James, with vastly superior forces, defeated Monmouth, who was captured, tried in London and beheaded.

"James took dire retribution against all those who had supported Monmouth. He sent out a judge, known as 'Bloody Judge Jeffreys,' whose job it was to track down all supporters of Monmouth, who were then hanged. He was already very unpopular and also, under his regime, the power of Parliament was cut down to such an extent that it was virtually non-existent.

"He was also very hard up – the Treasury was bare. So he persuaded my ancestor, the fourth Earl, to lend him thirty thousand pounds – a vast amount of money in those days. That was all right, but when he was asked to repay the loan, all he got was an IOU.

"Because of the treatment which had been given to the supporters of Monmouth, he became more and more universally hated. Henry VIII had decreed that all monarchs of Britain must be head of the Church of England; this meant that no Roman Catholic could be King or Queen of England.

"By this time, the landowners and the wealthy had had enough. A group, of which the fourth Earl was one of the leaders, decided to get rid of him. The scheme was that they should secretly invite his daughter, who was married to William of Orange, of the Netherlands, to become Queen, William to become Regent. They were both staunch Protestants. William would have none of it. He would only agree provided there was a joint monarchy – William and Mary. This was agreed.

"The plan was for the forces of the plotters to encircle the outskirts of London, and for an armed fleet with William and Mary aboard to sail up the Thames with bands playing and demand that James abdicate. It was anticipated that the people of London would flock to acclaim them. The fleet assembled in the Netherlands and sailed across the North Sea in the direction of the Thames.

"The thing was a fiasco: the wind blew in the wrong direction, and the ships couldn't sail up the Thames. They were blown down the Channel. They were in a very sorry state and sought shelter in Torbay, here in Devon. A very bedraggled William and Mary managed to make shore here at Brixham, and come up the steps where you have just seen his statue."

"Go on – tell me what happened next," said Kick.

"Well, James, when he heard the news, like a fool, instead of sitting tight in London sallied forth with a body of troops to slaughter the party which was making its way from the West Country towards London. But James soon found that his troops did not think much of the situation at all. He did not have the money to pay them: they all started to desert him.

"Meanwhile, the Earl and his supporters calmly marched into London and re-established themselves as Parliament.

"By now James, in the West Country, found himself virtually abandoned. All his troops had walked out on him. He headed back to London, only to be faced with a *fait accompli.* He was told that he was to abdicate; he would be given a pension, subject to him living abroad and never returning to Britain. William and Mary arrived in London, were acclaimed by everyone and, in due course, crowned King and Queen. They showered favours on all those who had made all this possible, and in gratitude they made my ancestor, the fourth Earl, the first Duke of Devonshire. James tried to regain the throne by raising an army in Ireland, but William went over and, in the Battle of the Boyne defeated his Roman Catholic troops with a British Protestant army. James fled back to the Continent, where he spent the rest of his life in exile."

"Bill, if someone were to write this as fiction I would think it was too farfetched to be true."

"Well, it's true all right – that's how we became Dukes. After all that, I could do with another drink, then we'd better get going if we want to get back to town before the blackout. Are you sure you're not bored with this? I feel like a ruddy history teacher."

"No Bill, honestly; I must know," she replied, "I must know."

24

Bill and Kick entered into the final stages of the election campaign with great gusto. He was very keen to follow the family tradition and enter into the political arena. After all, this was the family seat, almost by right. Kick followed him around, waving her large blue rosette with great enthusiasm. He had received a letter from Churchill. The Prime Minister sent his good wishes for the campaign, he was sure that the voters would show their loyalty to himself by voting for Bill as their MP. This was loudly cheered when Bill read it out, which he did at the meetings on every possible occasion.

There was, to their surprise, a lack of enthusiasm from some of the voters. Hartington came in for quite a few snide remarks as to why he had left the army to fight the election. Their husbands and sons were in the services. It was not said, but did he do it to get out of the fighting? He should have stayed with his unit and fought with the rest of them, and not sought election until the war was over. He argued that he could do more for his country by serving them in Parliament than by staying in the army.

His opponent, the Labour candidate, was a local man, well respected and well liked. But of course, with Churchill running the country – the great leader – there could not be any doubt that the candidate whom he supported –

Hartington – would be elected. However, his opponent had conducted a very visible and enthusiastic campaign amongst the working classes in the district, and seemed to have received quite a lot of support.

Polling day was a day of great excitement. Everyone, including Kick, rushed around to try and see that everyone went to the polls.

They were all assembled on the stage of the local Town Hall to await the result. It was going to be a great celebration. But it was a disaster – Hartington had lost, and by over 5,000 votes. It seemed that the voters had decided that they no longer had a duty to support the privileged class of the country. The days of the respect that had to be shown to the great landowners, the titled owners of inherited wealth, were past.

The whole family was astonished at the result. When news of the defeat was received by Churchill, he took it as a personal affront: how could they possibly not support his candidate when they must know that it was he who was leading the country to eventual victory?

The result meant, of course, that Bill would now come off the Army Reserve and would be called up to rejoin his unit. They decided that they could wait no longer. Bill and Kick agreed that they should get married as soon as possible. The Devonshires were very fond of Kick, and the Duke gave his consent to the marriage – with one proviso. Bill would not be allowed to join the Roman Catholic Church, and any children must be brought up as members of the Church of England. They both agreed – but the reaction of the Kennedys was soon forthcoming and was as expected.

"You tell me that the Devonshires have agreed that you can marry Hartington – well, I tell you that this marriage cannot take place," said Joe "You have been brought up in the true faith – the Roman Catholic Church. You have vowed to comply with all the rules and regulations of our faith and you know that we only marry members of our faith. Now you tell me that you can still remain a member of the Church, because the Devonshires have agreed, providing that any children be brought up as members of the Church of England. But this is fundamentally against the basic teaching of the RC faith – don't you see, it is quite impossible for this marriage to take place?"

"Don't you realise that to be married to Bill means more to me than anything else in the world?" replied Kick.

"So what do you want me to do – make an application to the Pope to give you dispensation and also to allow your children to be brought up in the Church of England faith? You know as well as I do that there is no possible chance that he would consider doing this for one moment,", said Joe. "The Dukes of Devonshire throughout the centuries have always been closely associated with the Church of England. It is their tradition and they would not agree to change their minds and let my children be Roman Catholics."

"I am sorry, dear", said Rose, "that you are placed in this unhappy situation. I know how much you love Bill, and we like him very much, but there is no other solution to this problem. You will have to tell Bill that because of your differing beliefs you are unable to marry him."

"No, Mother," said Kick, "I shall not tell him that, because come what may I am going to marry Bill. I will remain a Roman Catholic but we agree that any children can be brought up in the Church of England. Do you realise what you are expecting me to do? Give up Bill whom I love so much, give up being Lady Hartington and give up one day being the Duchess of Devonshire."

"This is quite absurd," said Joe. "If you persist I shall consider cutting off your allowance, but that's beside the point. Unless you are married in a Roman Catholic Church, then the Church would not consider you properly married."

"But if I married outside the Church I would be properly and legally married, wouldn't I, Father?" said Kick.

"So that's how it is," replied Joe sourly. "Despite all we have done for you, have you no consideration as to how this will look to all our friends and, for that matter, to the public? I tell you, girl, if you do as you say I shall forbid any member of the family to attend your wedding, whenever it is."

Rose followed Joe out of the room. She had such mixed feelings: she knew that Joe was right, they must respect the terms of the Church in which they had both been brought up and which they had brought up the children. But she felt so strongly for Kick and, to be fair, for how much she was to miss the sort of wedding she had always dreamed of for Kick. And behind it all she had to admit to herself it would really be something if Kick were to become Lady Hartington.

Joe Junior found Kick in tears. He put his arms round her shoulders, "How did it go, Kick?" he said.

"It was terrible. Father insists I give up Bill – I'm in a turmoil, I hardly know what to do."

"But you do, don't you?" said Joe.

"Yes, of course, Joe," she smiled through her tears, "I'm going to marry him. Father is threatening to cut off my allowance and he says that he will forbid any member of the family to attend the wedding."

"Well, Kick – there's one person who will attend your wedding – that's me, you can take that for certain."

Kick smiled, "Oh thanks, Joe, thanks, that's wonderful." She turned and kissed him.

"We do seem to make life difficult for ourselves, don't we?" said Joe. "The old man will go through the roof when he gets to know about Mary – not only is she a Protestant but she is still married. We shall have to get over that hurdle somehow – I want to marry her and I know she wants to marry me."

Bill and Kick's wedding was very different to the sort of wedding that was traditional for the heir of the Devonshires, usually grand affairs at St Margarets or St Pauls, attended by all the titled members of the establishment, in the past even royalty. They were married at the Chelsea Registry Office, with only a handful of people in attendance. Joe Junior was best man. This was, however, followed by a terrific wedding party for over 200 held at the home of a close friend in the West End of London.

25

Prior to the wedding, following his failure to get elected to Parliament, Bill had been recalled to join his unit with the Coldstream Guards. He had managed to get a week's leave for the wedding and his honeymoon. They decided to spend the time at their favourite place, Compton Place, one of the very few houses belonging to the Devonshires that had not been requisitioned by the army.

They were sitting in the grounds drinking coffee.

"So now you've married me you've got two Americans in the family," said Kick.

"You mean Adèle," replied Bill.

"Now that she has been recently widowed, how is she getting on?"

"It was good of her to come across to our wedding, but I didn't have much time to talk to her," said Bill. "It's only about a month since Uncle Charles died, but she said that she was OK. For the time being she is staying at Lismore. You know why he died (he was quite young) – he was a lush. We were amazed when we learned that she had agreed to marry him.

"As you know, she and her brother Fred were the toast of the London stage – Fred and Adèle Astaire. Their dancing in shows such as *Funny Face* used to bring the house down. She used to complain that Fred, who was a quiet chap, demanded that she practised all his new dance routines with him every day, when she wanted to go out and enjoy herself

I was in my teens when I used to go and meet them backstage. I thought it was great. She met up with Charles and his set, and they did the rounds, enjoying themselves, but of course he drank like a fish. We never seemed to see him without a glass in his hand. It was difficult. I heard on the grapevine that Father did everything he could to put her off marrying him. The whole family had tried to stop him drinking without success – but Adèle had made up her mind. She said she would cure him of the habit.

She married him and became Lady Charles Cavendish. We all wondered how Fred would feel losing her as his partner: they were a terrific team. But he's now back in America, making as big a name for himself as he did over here.

It seemed strange that she decided to give all that up to go and live in the centre of Ireland in a medieval castle – Lismore – it's quite a dump. What happens is that, as you know, we have several large properties and houses: each member of the family is allocated to one. Charles took over Lismore and the management of the seventy thousand acres of land and the properties we own around it. By all accounts, Adèle soon started to knock the old castle into shape. The locals had never met anyone like her before: a famous actress – an American. By all accounts they thought the world of her. It's a great pity that it had to end as it did. I don't think that she will want to live permanently in that great rambling place; still, it's early days – perhaps she'll go back to the States."

"What I can't understand, Bill, is how your family have come to own all this land and all these properties all over the place," said Kick.

"The dynasty, if that's the right word, was founded way back at the time of Henry VIII, and it wasn't founded by any knight on the battlefield but by a girl – a most amazing character, whose name has gone down in history as Bess of Hardwick. She was the daughter of a farmer who owned a few acres of land in Derbyshire. At the age of thirteen they married her off to a delicate young boy who lived at the farm next door. This did not last long, as he died inside twelve months. The family were so hard up that they sent her off as a kind of unpaid help to the home of a distant rich relative named La Zouche in London. As they were quite wealthy, she was able to mix with a very different type of person from that she had on the farm, and after two years she met a middle-aged widower named William Cavendish. Now, his family were quite well-connected at Court, and this was at the time when Henry VIII was having a hell of a row with the Pope because he wouldn't let him divorce his wife Katherine, so Henry decided to break with the Roman Catholic Church – he would have one of his own, so he founded the Church of England.

"William Cavendish's father managed to get for him the job of King's accountant. He was not the sort of accountant who looks after your tax. His job was to transfer all the wealth of the Roman Church – all the properties and the land – throughout a large area of the Midlands to the newly formed Church of England. So over the years he and Bess raised their family, and during this time, he managed to acquire for himself large areas of land in Derbyshire and the surrounding district. Bess, by this time, had great visions of grandeur; she persuaded him to build a large mansion in Derbyshire, which they named Chatsworth. This was all right whilst Henry VIII and his son Edward were on the throne, but when his daughter

Mary came to the throne as Queen Mary I, life became very different. She was a staunch Roman Catholic and became known as Bloody Mary.

"She set out to recoup for the Roman Church some of their losses. She had investigations made as to how the wealthy landowners had acquired their wealth, and one who came under the closest scrutiny was William Cavendish. After holding the enquiries at bay for quite a long time, the axe fell. He was accused of misappropriating Crown funds and land for his own use. He was to stand trial at Court, but in the meantime to pay a fine of five thousand pounds. However, before he was tried he very conveniently died. The Queen decided that they would not accuse Bess of being implicated but she must pay the fine. Bess was in despair; this would have ruined her – it was a vast amount of money at that time. It seemed that all her dreams of grandeur were shattered.

Then, by sheer luck, Bloody Mary died and her stepsister Elizabeth came to the throne. Now, during Mary's reign Elizabeth had been kept very much in the background, away from Court, as Mary did not want the very strong Protestant lobby to use her as a foil to weaken her authority. She had been pushed around the country to stay at various houses, and from time to time Bess had been called upon to look after her. Bess hurried to London and, crying her eyes out, pleaded with her to help her in her sad plight. In view of the way she had looked after her in the past, Elizabeth, who was not known for her generosity, did agree to help and told her she could pay the fine over a long period.

"So, with joy in her heart, Bess returned to Chatsworth and, with the help of her second son William and his wife, settled down to administer and build up the estates. She had disowned her eldest son, who was known locally as the Ram of Derbyshire.

"Although by all accounts she was no great beauty, she must have had something, because within two years she married her near neighbour, the very elegant Sir William Lowe, the Captain of the Queen's Guard, the owner of large areas of land in the Midlands. He treated her very well; he paid off all her debts and then, after a comparatively short period of time, he conveniently died. She inherited all his estates. By this time she was very wealthy, well-known and accepted at Court. Her son had taken his father's title as Sir William Cavendish.

"Now, a large portion of her land was adjacent to that of the Earl of Shrewsbury, who was a widower. So after another couple of years she married him. Poor old Shrewsbury – he didn't know what he was letting himself in for. She made sure before they were married that all her estates would be inherited by her heirs. But as Shrewsbury's wife, she charged up all the running costs of her properties and land to him: he didn't appreciate it at all.

"The Queen had made Shrewsbury responsible for the safe custody of her cousin, Mary Queen of Scots, who had plotted against her. She was kept under guard in various country houses but, as a Queen, Mary demanded that she be treated in accordance with her rank, and kept her staff and retinue with her at all times. But when Shrewsbury sent to Elizabeth the bills for the cost of maintaining her and her court, as well as the cost of the guards, she conveniently forgot to pay him.

After terrific arguments with Bess about the payment of all her bills, the poor chap got so fed up he walked out on her.

Meanwhile, Bess had built for herself a beautiful house, which of course we still own – Hardwick Hall. She handed over Chatsworth to her heir and installed herself in the new house, from where, after the death of Shrewsbury, she sued his successors for her fair share, as his wife, of his estates. Just before she died, at a ripe old age, by which time she was one of the richest persons in the land, the two families were reconciled."

"What a story," said Kick.

"Yes, that's how it all started," he replied.

"Tell me – if the family own all these estates in the centre of England, what do you own in Devonshire?"

"We don't own anything."

"Well, how did you come to get the title of Devonshire?"

"Are you sure you want me to go on?"

"Of course I do," she demanded.

"Very well; but first of all, let's get Mrs Rawlins to bring out some tea. Give me a break – I'm getting thirsty," he replied.

26

After they had been served with their tea, they settled down and he continued with his saga.

"The story goes that, when Elizabeth died and James VI of Scotland became James I of England, he found life very difficult: the Treasury was bare. It seemed that all the wealth of the country was in the hands of the landowning Earls and Lords. So, working on the basis that if you can't beat 'em join 'em, he advised the wealthiest of the Lords that he felt that, in view of their standing in the land, he should honour them by making them Earls.

"By this time Sir William Cavendish had been made Lord Cavendish. All lords had to do was to confirm that they would be honoured to accept this the title of Earl and to forward to him, for the honour, the sum of ten thousand pounds – a huge amount at that time. So my ancestor duly jumped on the bandwagon: he raised the ten thousand and forwarded the cash to the Treasury. But when the clerk at Court came to prepare the letters patent, it's said that he couldn't read the handwriting and instead of making him the Earl of Derbyshire he was made the Earl of Devonshire."

Kick laughed. "Is that really true?"

"Well," said Bill, "that's the way the story goes; it's supposed to be true. That's enough – drink up your tea."

They decided to go into the town, some 15 minutes walk away, to look around the shops and then, after dinner, they settled down to their coffee in the lounge.

"Bill, I don't want to be a bore, but will you tell me the rest of the family history?" said Kick.

"All right," said Bill. "I've already told you how the fourth Earl became the first Duke. Well, he decided that he would build up all the properties on the estates, and in particular Chatsworth – he made it the size of a small palace. His son, the second Duke, was a great soldier, but when he settled down he found the walls of the houses particularly cold and bare, so he decided that he would cover them as much as possible with pictures. He got the collecting bug and started the collection of the works of art that we own today. The cost at that time was of course peanuts compared with what they are worth today.

"His son, the third Duke, was a great gambler and always short of ready cash, so he did it the easy way: he married the daughter of one of the richest financiers in the city. She brought in a very substantial dowry. We may be one of the wealthiest property and landowners in the country, but the cost of managing them is enormous – ready cash has always been very welcome. But the fourth Duke really hit the jackpot.

"The original Earls of Burlington had been involved in a terrific family feud as to who should inherit the vast family wealth. They owned Lismore Castle in Ireland and all the adjoining land, Burlington House in the centre of London, Chiswick House, a great mansion in parkland in West London, and large areas of land in Yorkshire. The family feud resulted in the title dying out, and the whole of the estates were inherited by the Earl's daughter, Lady Charlotte Boyle. The Duchess was horrified when she learned that her son was going to marry into such a disreputable family and did everything she could to stop it, but apparently it was quite a successful marriage and added fabulous wealth to the family.

"His brother, George Cavendish, also did very well for himself. The Earl of Northampton had acquired for himself large areas around London, in Kent and along the Sussex coast. How he got them was a bit suspect. He did not have a son and only one daughter, Lady Elizabeth Compton. She inherited everything, and George married her, and of course came to own everything. Now, as the title of the Earl of Burlington had died out he managed to get himself made the first Earl of Burlington – second edition. Haven't you had enough?"

"No," said Kick, "it sounds more like the story in a novel than a true history."

"All right then. The fifth Duke married into the very wealthy and titled Spencer family – Lady Georgina Spencer. Her great interest in life was gambling. You know where the Ritz Hotel is in Piccadilly? At that time there was, opposite, our great London home – Devonshire House, a large rambling place, and here Georgina arranged her great gambling parties for all the important people of the day, including royalty. The Duke got so fed up with her addiction and her debts that he installed his girlfriend into the house to provide him with some home comforts whilst she got on with her gambling.

"After an inordinate length of time she did, to everyone's relief, provide a son and heir, who of course became the sixth Duke. You remember I told you about him – the Bachelor Duke, who added to our already vast collection of works of art. When he died, everything was inherited by the second Earl of Buckingham who, already very wealthy in his own right, became the seventh Duke and inherited everything. As I've already told you, he created Eastbourne.

"Well, I think that fills you in all about the family. You now know what you have let yourself in for. I'm back with my unit in a couple of days. Goodness knows when we shall be here together again."

Kick was finally realising the vast wealth and power of the family into which she had married.

27

The honeymoon over, Bill rejoined his unit, and for a short time Kick was able to find accommodation near where he was stationed. The country was now ready for the great day. There was now a Commander-in-Chief for all the forces in Europe – the American General Dwight Eisenhower. The intensity of the German night bombing had dropped off, but Hitler had found a deadly weapon to launch against the population: the flying bomb – a pilot-less plane. The engines of these machines cut out when they were over their target and crashed, the bombs they carried causing appalling destruction and death.

The distinctive noise of their engines became known to everyone, who waited fearfully, hoping that the flying bomb would pass overhead: if the engine cut out everyone dived for shelter, hoping that the cursed thing would not crash near to them.

* * *

"Kick – is that you? This is Joe."

"Oh Joe – great to hear from you. How are you?"

"I'm fine. Listen – I've managed to get a weekend leave and have booked a room for us at the Savoy. Is it possible for you and Bill to get off at the same time, so that the four of us can meet up?"

"OK. I'll contact Bill to see if he can make it – when?"

"The weekend after next," he said.

"Very well. I'll phone you back and let you know if that's OK."

Both Bill and Kick were curious to meet Joe Junior's girlfriend Mary. Bill managed to get a weekend leave, and they met in the bar at the Savoy, neither Kick nor Bill commenting on the wedding ring on Mary's finger. It was a good party. They had finished dinner – "Where shall we go?" said Bill.

"Where do you want to go?" asked Kick.

"Let's go to the Windmill," he suggested.

Kick laughed. "Now that's just about the high level of entertainment we would expect from you two. Do you really expect us to sit amongst a crowd of goggle-eyed lechers cheering the dancing girls – the nudes – the corny comedians?"

They were still arguing as to where to go when the dreaded air-raid warning sounded. "Damn," said Bill. "If the thing comes down here, there's nothing we can do about it. Let's risk it – let's stay here."

The dining room was emptying. The head waiter came hurrying across. "I'm sorry, My Lord," he said, "I have to close the restaurant. It's the rule – everyone must go to the shelter."

"Well, I suppose we have to go," said Joe. "You can't blame them – you know what happened at the Café de Paris. There were three hundred down there enjoying themselves – they bought it – a direct hit killed the lot."

They made their way to the shelter via the private entrance at the rear of the hotel. The shelter was already very full, the public coming in from the Embankment entrance. They managed to get a couple of seats for the girls and indulged in small talk, hoping that the all-clear would soon be sounded – now very different from earlier in the war, when the bombing raids kept people in the shelters all night.

"Friends, friends – may I have your attention please." A tall young priest, dressed in a black robe, his large gold cross on his chest, stood up and addressed the crowd. "Friends, I am sure that you will wish to join me in a prayer to the Lord, to pray for the safety of all those assembled here and the safety of those who have been unable to seek shelter."

"Everyone shuffled to their feet and self-consciously bowed their heads. He began: "Oh Lord, we pray . . ."

A snort sounded across the shelter. "You hypocrite – you bloody hypocrite." They were stunned as a distraught, middle-aged, well-dressed man shouted from the back of the room. "You pray to a God of love who is supposed to control the lives of all mankind. What sort of a God allows a German plane to bomb and kill my wife, my daughter, her two young children? What sort of a God makes my son a hero to bomb and murder innocent German men, women and children? What sort of a God allows us to cower here, waiting to be indiscriminately slaughtered? Is that your God? If there was a God, a Christ, how could he allow this slaughter – this inhumanity of man to man? You hypocrite – you can have your God."

He pushed his way through the crowd to the exit and out into the night. There was a stunned silence. The priest held his hands in prayer. "Friends, we have heard the cry of a poor misguided man. Let us pray: let us pray that the Lord will forgive him for . . ."

Suddenly the all-clear sounded. The embarrassed crowd hurried to the exits, leaving the priest in prayer.

The four returned to the bar. The incident soon seemed forgotten – they had other things to think about. After saying goodnight to Bill and Kick, Joe and Mary made their way to their room.

"Joe," said Mary, "Can we talk?"

"Are you all right?" he said. "You seem very quiet. Did that fellow in the shelter upset you?"

"Not really: but what about us, Joe, what about our religions? All your family are such staunch Catholics. Here I am, a married woman. I want a divorce – I want to marry you, I love you so much, I want us to have children," she said.

"Of course I want to marry you: I *will* marry you," said Joe. "When you've got your divorce, I'm sure I can get a dispensation from Rome to allow us to marry."

"For you to do that, Joe, wouldn't that only be given subject to me becoming a Catholic?"

"Well," he said, "I suppose it would."

"The point is, Joe, that it doesn't matter. I've always gone to Church – C of E – but it doesn't matter any more. I would be prepared to become a Catholic, but I would only pay lip service. I would do it only because I want to spend my life with you – it would mean nothing to me. If our children had to be brought up in the Roman Catholic faith I would agree, but one day I would tell them that they must make up their minds what they believed in, not what people tell them to believe. My heart went out to that man in the shelter. His life has been ruined – can you blame him for being such a sceptic? I want to live, Joe, to live with you – that's all that matters."

Joe turned to her, kissed her – what could he say? He loved her more than he had realised.

28

The Allied Forces now virtually had air supremacy: fighter planes on constant patrol, seeking to intercept the flying bombs. They succeeded in shooting down quite a number, but the majority still got through.

In Italy, the Allied Forces had broken out of their bridgeheads on the western coast and were making their way northwards. The German resistance in central Italy was crumbling. As the Allies approached Rome, the Germans evacuated the city: it was declared an open city. The population turned out in their thousands to cheer and greet the entry of their former enemies. Italy was in a state of chaos. Fascism was finished.

The news from Rome was overshadowed by that of the following day – 6 June – the day that everyone had been waiting for: the invasion of the Continent of Europe by the Allied Forces – D-Day.

Numerous devices and red herrings had been used to keep the Germans from knowing exactly where the forces would land. The obvious places were by the shortest route, directly across the Channel. Hitler had assembled a major defence force in that area, but the Allies landed in massive force in the region of the Cherbourg Peninsula. The British troops succeeded in securing a bridgehead, suffering far lower casualties than had been anticipated, but the

American troops, landing a little further along the coast to the west, met massive opposition and, before gaining their foothold, suffered very heavy casualties.

Bill Hartington's unit of the Coldstream Guards followed the initial landings. The whole of Britain and America waited with bated breath to hear whether the great gamble had succeeded. British and American forces fighting their way inland joined forces, and a great battle raged around the French town of Caen.

With more and more men and equipment now pouring across the Channel, the Allies were now fully established on the Continent. Then the German defences crumbled – they retreated at speed back eastwards across the north of France to defend their homeland.

Kick, like all wives, waited anxiously for news of Bill. To her delight, she heard that he was safe. His unit – he was now a Major – was chasing the Germans across the north of France as they retreated towards Brussels. It was a hayride – they had the greatest difficulty in keeping up with them.

29

On 18 August news came that the Allies had landed on the south coast of France, encountering very little opposition, and then, to the great jubilation of the whole of France, Allied forces, led by General De Gaulle leading the Free French forces, marched into Paris. Paris had been made an open city: the inhabitants went wild.

Kick was thrilled with the letter she had received from Bill, "It was terrific, Kick," he wrote. "We were instructed to march on Brussels, news had come in that the Germans were evacuating the city. As we marched in the last of the Germans had pulled out and I led the first of the Allied forces into the city. The people went mad – cheering, throwing flowers – the welcome was unbelievable. They had been under Nazi rule for over four years, they were overwhelmed with joy. I eagerly await your letters and hope to have some news from you. Your ever loving Bill.'

She placed the letter with those she had previously received from him – she was so very happy with the marriage, marred only by the fact that prior to and now a short time since he had left England there was no sign of her being pregnant.

The Allies launched a paratroop invasion of Holland. It was completely successful – the Germans retreated. The great port of Antwerp was now available to the Allies to service their troops. It looked as if the war was almost over – but it was not to be.

Whereas in the earlier part of the war the cities of Britain were heavily bombed by the Luftwaffe, the boot was now on the other foot. Fleets of heavy RAF bombers at night and fleets of American Flying Fortresses by day dropped hundreds of tons of their deadly cargo over the industrial cities of Germany. The damage done was indescribable.

Britain was now suffering from the terror of the pilotless flying bombs, and British Intelligence had received news that Hitler had boasted that he now had a secret weapon that would be launched against Britain, which was so devastating that, despite the defeats on land, the Allies would have to sue for peace. They had learned that the secret weapon was a gigantic rocket packed with high explosives, which could be launched from sites well away from the fighting zones. It was known as the V2. They were to be launched in their thousands. They could reach any city in Britain: there was absolutely no defence against them. Due to the rapid advance of the Allied forces, some of the launching pads had been overrun, but the Allies knew of many more out of reach, except by air.

The experiments in which Joe Junior had been involved at the secret base in Essex were designed to find a way of delivering a single load of such high explosive on a pin-pointed target that it would be completely demolished. The threat of the V2 rockets had resulted in the High Command deciding that these were to be the priority targets. Intelligence was sending in details of where they were being made and of the secret launching pads.

Their fear was fully justified. Early in November the first of the V2s landed on London. There was no warning – no chance of taking cover. They had a colossal explosive charge. The area where it landed was completely demolished.

Joe Junior's unit had perfected their method of counter-attacking this menace. They were stripping out of a number of Lancaster bombers all possible equipment and armament to reduce the weight – everything other than what was needed to fly the plane. The planes were packed with explosives – in fact flying bombs. The only crew was to be the pilot – he would not even have a navigator. The plane would be escorted to the target by a squadron of fighters, and they would give him the signal to crash-land the plane on the target and the point when he should eject by parachute after he had switched on the electric charges. Two or three successful missions had been made and two of the pilots were known to have landed safely.

They were sitting in the tiny lounge of their cottage after having their lunch, drinking coffee. "I'm detailed to report back to base this evening on standby", said Joe, "I'll kip down in the mess overnight."

"Standby – does that mean you may be operational?" Mary went cold as she asked.

"Yes, maybe," he said – it was not maybe, he knew that he would be going. What went on at the airport was top secret – Mary had heard rumours in the village that work was being done on super-sized bombs, but there was no real information. Joe had never told her what he was really engaged on, but she was very apprehensive. God, don't let anything happen to him.

"Let's spend a little time upstairs this afternoon, Mary," he said.

"Whenever you like, Joe," she replied, putting her arm through his and leading the way.

Joe stepped out of the Jeep which had brought him from the mess across the tarmac to the great looming mass of the Lancaster. As he climbed aboard the plane loaded with all the gear and parachute, he felt that all eyes were on him. He had no illusions – his plane was nothing more than a flying bomb. He was not worried about parachuting – he had had plenty of practice. Where you landed was the luck of the draw. Waiting for him to settle down in the cock-pit was Station Chief Engineer. Between them they checked every switch gauge and all gadgets – particularly the leavers he would operate so that seconds after he had exited from the plane, the whole mass of explosives which virtually filled the plane would explode on the target at which it had been directed. The Chief Engineer gave him the OK, wished him best of luck and climbed out of the plane, leaving Joe feeling as though he was alone in the world. He was given instructions to take off, and he knew that his fighter escort would follow him as soon as he was airborne and take up their positions to protect him from enemy planes. His take-off was smooth and uneventful. Over the sea he was joined by his fighter escorts. Over the intercom he received instructions to check the detonating safety device on the bomb mechanism. As he did so the whole world exploded – the force was so great that the escorting fighters were blown off course – the plane fragmented and what was left fell and sank into the sea leaving only bits and pieces to float away. There was no possibility of tracing Joe's remains.

30

Kick, back on duty with the American Red Cross, was quite a celebrity with the GIs. She enjoyed the way they wanted to talk with her, dance with her, tell her of their wives and sweethearts, show her snapshots of their families. They wrote home all about the titled lady who would one day be a Duchess: they didn't have those sort of ladies with titles in the States.

When off-duty, she was able to enjoy the use of the Devonshire's London home. Often her in-laws were away at the house the Duke liked best – Compton Place. The Duke, a handyman, liked nothing better than to potter about the grounds and gardens and in the vegetable and fruit garden which supplied a lot of their needs.

After coming off-duty one evening, she had gone back to the house when the phone rang.

"It's for you, my lady," called the maid. "The American Embassy." She picked up the phone.

"Is that Lady Hartington?"

"Yes," she replied.

"This is Charles Ruston from the embassy, Lady Hartington." She knew him quite well. "I'm sorry to say that I have some very bad news for you," he said. Her heart stood still. Bill – she waited with bated breath. "You see, your brother Joe was engaged in some very dangerous flying duties. I'm sorry that I have to tell you that the plane he was piloting on a mission to Germany exploded in mid-air – he was killed immediately. There's no trace of his body."

She was rooted to the spot. Thank God it wasn't Bill. But Joe – the one member of her family she was really close to, who always took her side – her confidant. Recovering! she said, "Have the embassy informed my parents?"

"Yes," he replied. "We were able to contact them before we phoned you. You can guess that they are most distressed. They said that they would like you to go home immediately."

"Oh yes, of course I will. Can you make the arrangements for me?"

"Yes, of course. I'll get you flown back to the States as soon as possible. I assume that you will contact your unit and get compassionate leave? I'll be back with you in the morning."

She thanked him. Replacing the receiver, she felt devastated. Her application for compassionate leave was a formality. Charles Ruston and her unit pulled out all the stops for her.

The next day, with the minimum of luggage, she was driven in an army jeep to the vast American Air Force base at Ruislip on the western perimeter of London and there she boarded a converted DC3 bomber used for transport work for the long, tedious and uncomfortable flight to the American Air Force base at Cambridge, not far from the family's home near Boston. The plane had to stop to be refuelled in Newfoundland. The crew had made her as comfortable as possible. There were six other passengers, three high-ranking officers and three badly wounded limbless GIs, who were being taken back home.

Feeling completely exhausted, she was relieved to find the family Cadillac waiting for her on the tarmac at the foot of the steps as she stepped off the plane to take her to the family home at Hyannis Point.

They were all there to greet her, united in their grief. Her mother kissed her affectionately – it was not the time to open up old wounds.

Her father was in the depths of despair.

"Why, why didn't he come home when he had the chance? All the things I had planned for him. Why did he stay in England when he had everything going for him here?" His dream that Joe Junior could one day become President of America was shattered.

Kick did not feel that it was the time to disillusion him; Joe had told her that if the family refused to accept him marrying a Protestant divorcée, he would do so come what may. He was adamant that he intended to marry her. He was prepared to sacrifice anything for that.

Joe went off to nurse his sorrows alone in his study. He had built up all his hopes for Joe Junior. He had everything – looks, a good sportsman, did well at Harvard, already liked in the political field, fitting right into the background of the family connections with the Irish-Americans. What a tragic waste.

Now what was he to do? There were Jack and Robert and, of course, Edward – not that he had much in the way of expectations for him. Could he build up Jack to take the place of his hopes for Joe? The snag was his health: when he was fit he looked fine – tall, good-looking. He looked like a film star: the ladies would go for him in a big way – and by all accounts, he was already going for them. Of course, he hadn't personality like Joe, but there was no reason why he could not be built up. He would see that he had all the backing there was if he went into the political field. The strain of political life was tremendous, but if FDR, in spite of his disabilities, could cope, why not Jack?

He, Joe Kennedy, had made up his mind that one day there would be a Kennedy in the White House. Now that there was no Joe – it would take time, but in due course he would see that it would be Jack, and if he could not make it, there was Bobby. He was still quite young – smaller than the other boys, but always determined to keep up with them. Bobby played his cards close to his chest, but behind his outwardly quiet nature he was as tough as his father. If he wanted something, he went for it. It was early days. He had the signs of being a leader: if his campaign for building up Jack failed there was always Bobby.

As for Edward – Teddy – the youngest; despite all his efforts he had failed to get him into Harvard. They wouldn't have him at any price. His main interests seemed to be enjoying himself and, young as he was, chasing girls. He was brash but quite good at shooting a line. But he didn't seem to be of the same calibre as his older brothers.

The memorial service for Joe was held at the local Roman Catholic church, near the family home, attended by vast numbers of friends and acquaintances. Message of condolence were received from the President and leading figures in the land.

Kick's presence in the church was of great interest. Had she really broken faith? Fancy being married in a registry office. Still, look who she had married. What would her children's religion be? Still, one day she would be a Duchess. She was the centre of gossip.

"Mother, this has been such a sad time for us all," said Kick. "All the children loved Joe, he was the leader of the pack, we went to him with all our troubles. He never let us down, and I know that Jack misses him the most – Joe supported him through all his illness. Of course we all knew that Joe was Father's favourite, and what hopes he had to build him up to the top of the tree in politics. Now he is going to do the same for Jack; let's hope that his health holds up, that Father will not push him too far. The reason I wanted to have a word with you, Mother, is that this is all over. I have decided that I shall be going back to London – I feel that I belong there. I shall be making the arrangements with my Red Cross Unit."

"But you can't, dear" said Rose. "Why should you go back to all that danger? We hear that the Germans have been sending over pilotless planes filled with explosives which just drop anywhere – and more rockets which drop from the sky, explode and do terrific damage and death: there is no need for you to go back to all that. Bill has gone back to his unit so it's not as if you will be with him. You must stay here – your Father will never agree to you going back."

"Mother, whatever he may have to say will not make any difference, I think that he now realises that he can no longer rule our lives for us."

In an attempt to placate her, Rose persuaded her to go with Joe on a shopping trip to New York. They booked in at the Waldorf. New York was a different world to what she had left. The whole of the city was ablaze with lights at night, compared with blacked-out London. There was no damage – everything was as if there was no war: no shortages, the whole of America going on as before. Only those touched by the conflict, those whose husbands or sons were serving thousands of miles away in the forces, of who had made the final sacrifice in the service of world peace, were affected and realised the horrors of war.

Returning from a shopping expedition with her mother, on entering the hotel Kick was informed by reception that there was a message from her father: would she phone him immediately. Joe came on the phone.

"Kick, our embassy in London have been trying to get in touch with you: they gave me a message. They've heard from the British War Office. I'm afraid it's the worst possible, Kick: Bill has been killed in action."

She was stunned. She could not remember replacing the receiver. Her whole world had crashed around her. Why had fate treated her like this? She had loved Bill. All their hopes and plans were in ashes. She was heart-broken.

31

Kick's journey back to London was a nightmare. After the dreadful news had sunk in, she and Rose hurried back home, where they learned of the arrangements that had been made for her to be flown back to London. Starting early the next morning, accompanied by her father, they were driven by their chauffeur through the beautiful New England countryside to Quebec. The weather was cold but dry. With the approach of winter the maple trees had shed most of their leaves but there were still enough left to add a scarlet tinge to the countryside.

Following a long journey, as darkness was approaching they pulled into the entrance of the vast RAF Transport Command complex on the outskirts of Quebec. After being checked at the gates they were driven to the officers' mess, where they were greeted by the Station Commander. The base was where new Lancaster bombers which had been manufactured in America and Canada were marshalled and then flown by RAF Transport air crews to Britain, there to be fully kitted out and armed and prepared for battle, to take their place amongst the bombers used with such devastating effect against the cities of Germany.

After thanking her host for all the trouble that had been taken on her behalf, Kick bade a tearful farewell to her father. She was taken out by Jeep to a brand new Lancaster which was being warmed up on the runway. The crew made her as comfortable as possible in the improvised cabin.

The flight was uneventful, tiring and tedious. After what seemed an interminable time, it eventually touched down at its home base in East Anglia.

The Duke and Duchess were waiting to meet her as she arrived.

"Kick," he said. "this is terrible news for you and for all of us." He put his arms around her shoulder. "We have lost our eldest son whom we loved so much, and you, after such a short time, have had Bill taken away from you."

"I am heartbroken," said Kick. "I expect that some people will have been saying that I married him for his title, but that is not true, we both loved each other so much, we were so happy together and it was for such a short time."

She was shown to her room and after she had freshened up, she joined the Duke and Duchess in their drawing room.

"Kick," he said, "I know that this is a very sad time but there is a very personal question which I am sure you realise I must ask – are you pregnant? It is vital for the family to know."

"I quite understand," said Kick, "I fully realise the importance of the question. I was about to tell you. No – I am not pregnant. Before I left them, I told my mother and father that I was not pregnant – they realise the importance of the answer. The only thing that worried us when Bill and I were together was that I had not become pregnant: he so wanted an heir."

"As you say," said the Duke, "this news means a lot to us

all. I will send out the news to Andrew, who you know is with his unit in Italy. He will now inherit the title and will from now on be Lord Hartington and his wife will be Lady Hartington – you of course will keep your title, Kick – you will continue to be Lady Kathleen Hartington so as not to confuse the issue. The financial arrangements and adjustments which will have to be made will be very complicated but you need have no worry on that score. I am sure that you will be more than satisfied with the final outcome."

Kick went to her room, exhausted. It was all over – there would never be a Kennedy Duke of Devonshire.

It was not until next morning, when they were sitting quietly together, that they told her how Bill had come to meet his death.

After the relief of Brussels Bill's company, No. 3 of the Coldstream Guards, was sent out to occupy a village to the east of the city. The Germans had, unknown to the advancing troops, laid on a heavy rearguard defence. The company were caught unawares and were subject to a terrific barrage. They suffered very heavy losses – no less than 25 per cent of their force – and were forced to make a tactical withdrawal. They reformed and, two days later, once more advanced to take on the enemy. Bill, wearing his cream-coloured macintosh, an act of bravado amongst Guards officers, led the attack, his figure standing out clearly amongst his men. The enemy had withdrawn, leaving behind two or three concealed snipers. One of the snipers picked out Bill and shot him: he died instantly.

Bill's body was flown back to London, where the funeral service was attended by some of the most important personages in the land and a vast horde of mourners. After the service the coffin was taken to a private train which, together with three hundred mourners, travelled to

Chatsworth, and there he was buried in the Devonshires' private cemetery on the estate.

The only important absentee at the funeral was his brother Andrew. He was a Major with his unit of the Coldstream Guards, fighting a desperate battle against the Germans in the mountains of northern Italy, where the Nazis were stubbornly holding the line. The news had been sent out to him – he was the new Lord Hartington, heir to the Duke of Devonshire. Just the one thing he did not want; but fate had taken a hand. One day he would be Duke, but fortunately his father was only in his early fifties. He felt that he would not have to assume the dukedom for many years to come.

Standing by the grave among many mourners, Kick felt isolated in her despair. The future she had visualised had not materialised. She was left with her title, Lady Kathleen Hartington, but already there were a new Lord Hartington and another Lady Hartington.

During her time with Bill, she had felt that she was part of the British scene, part of the British Establishment. Did she want to return to the States and once more be a member of the Kennedy clan and their way of life? No she was going to make her life in Britain.

32

As the Germans withdrew towards their own borders they put up a very strong resistance. British forces, under General Montgomery, were severely mauled in an attempt to capture Arnhem, and the American forces, under General "Blood and Guts" Patton, met terrific resistance in the Ardennes.

But in Russia it was a different story. After months of trying to capture the city of Stalingrad in far eastern Russia, the Germans were completely routed and a whole army had to surrender. The Russians had started their relentless drive westwards.

The American political scene suffered a severe blow on 12 April, with the news of the sudden death of President Roosevelt. He and Churchill had, between them, been the main architects of the war. The free world owed him a debt of gratitude. By now the Americans were forcing the Japanese to give up and retreat from the Pacific islands they had conquered – but at no small cost.

In recapturing their original base in the Pacific, the island of Guadalcanal, the American Forces were faced with entrenched Japanese do-or-die defenders. The fighting was horrific, and the American nation paid tribute to the gallantry of their troops who, despite appalling losses sustained during the invasion, finally reoccupied the island.

As the Russians reached the outskirts of Berlin, Hitler realised that all was lost and in his bomb-proof shelter, together with Eva Braun, the woman he had just married, and Goebbels and his family, committed suicide by taking poison.

On 4 May General Montgomery, on behalf of the Allies, accepted the Germans' unconditional surrender. 8 May was a great day for the British – celebrated as VE Day. After all those years of agony, the war in Europe was at last over.

Japan, reeling from the might of the American Forces, was given the chance to surrender. They made no reply, and on 7 August two of the new type of bombs – atomic bombs – were dropped on the cities of Nagasaki and Hiroshima. The force of these explosions brought a new dimension to global war.

The Japanese capitulated and General MacArthur, Commander-in-Chief Allied Forces in the Pacific, arrived in Tokyo to accept their unconditional surrender.

At last the fighting was over. The countries looked back and licked their wounds. The job of reconstruction was going to be a gigantic one.

33

After the end of the war, with life returned to normal, Jack took a trip to London and was immediately taken ill. He had to stay in a London hospital for six months with agonising back trouble. The state of his health was something the family kept quiet about. On his return home to convalesce, he and his father got together to decide his future.

"Glad to see you looking so much better," Joe grabbed Jack affectionately by the arm.

"I'm feeling fine, said Jack, "except for the odd twinge in my back – just fine. I wanted to talk with you, Pa. Joe and I were such pals and I was never jealous of the way you were paving the way for him with the party and hoping that one day he might even make it to the White House – and now of course this can never be. While I have been laid up, Pa, I have been thinking. I am now feeling so much fitter and I want to go into politics. I am sure I am up to it."

Joe beamed – this was what he had hoped would happen, as soon as he had recovered from the news of Joe's death. Instead of him having to lead up to the issue with Jack, Jack himself had come forward and said he virtually wished to take Joe's place – it was great news.

"Jack, if that's what you want, then that's what I want for

you. I'll support you in every way – pull all the strings, meet everyone that matters, address the right meetings, cement our relationship with the Irish-Americans – with your appearance and personality you've got it made."

Joe went off to tell Rose. He was over the moon – he was back on track – he'd do everything he could for Jack. One day perhaps, there would be a Kennedy in the White House.

In April 1946 Jack announced that he intended to fight the seat of the English Congress District in Massachusetts. His father virtually ran the campaign. The whole family pitched in, including the redoubtable John Fitzgerald, his grandfather. His younger brother Bobby was involved one hundred per cent; he was feeling his feet, beginning to have political ambitions himself.

A great party was held before the election. It was alleged to have cost Joe 200,000 dollars. At the party Jack, on behalf of his father, handed over a cheque for 600,000 dollars to set up a school for Catholic children in Brighton. Jack was elected with a massive majority: he was on his way.

Initially he did not make much progress in Congress, but women drooled over him: he was handsome, tall, young, a man of the future. They went for him in a big way. And he was a chaser – of not so chaste ladies.

During the recess he went to Europe on a fact-finding Congressional mission. America was considering the implications of the Marshall Plan – to provide American money (vast amounts of money) to assist the countries of Europe to recover from the devastation of war. He broke his journey in Ireland, where he joined Kick, who was staying as a guest of the Devonshires at Lismore Castle, County Waterford. This was picture-book country. Kick had been invited to stay as long as she liked.

Jack arrived in time to attend a very large party which Kick had arranged and which included many well-known and important personalities, including Anthony Eden, who in time became British Prime Minister. Jack lost no time in cultivating him.

"Kick, I've been checking up on our Irish forebears and found out that they originally lived in a village named Ross, and it's no great distance from here – do you think I could get hold of a car and see if I can trace them?"

"I'll see what I can do," she said. She caught up with him later on in the day. "You're lucky – one of the stewards on the the estate says you may borrow his for the day – you'd better be careful, it's a bit of a banger. You can tip him when you get back."

Starting shortly after breakfast, driving through country lanes, Jack followed the rather vague instructions he had been given and finally struck the lane leading to the village of Ross. He parked outside what appeared to be the village store. Going inside he addressed the old woman behind the counter.

"I wonder if you could help me," he said. "I am a visitor from America and I am inquiring whether anyone named Kennedy lives around here."

"From America, why would you want to know about anyone of that name?" she demanded.

Jack gave her a dazzling smile – when Jack smiled, everybody smiled. "I think my ancestors came from this village, you see, my name is Kennedy."

"Now that is just wonderful," said the old woman, "just wonderful. Fancy you coming all the way from America. Well I've lived here all my life and when I was a little girl there were three or four families named Kennedy living in farms around the village, but they have all except just one gone – my mother said mostly to America, sometimes to join relatives who had already emigrated there. Bill Kennedy and his wife have a smallholding about three miles away, I'm sure that they would be ever so pleased to meet you. My goodness, this is interesting, ever so interesting, let me show you which way to go." Coming round from the counter she joined him at the door and gave him such detailed instructions that in a short time he reached the small thatched cottage which was obviously his destination.

Jack knocked on the door, which was opened by a large middle-aged lady, very much a farmer's wife.

Jack started to explain who he was. It seemed to take her a few minutes to get the gist of what he was saying, but when she did, she ushered him inside and went to get her husband who was working in the yard.

The farmer, Bill Kennedy, and his wife sat open-mouthed as Jack explained just who the Kennedy family in America were – how his father was a senator in the government in Washington, how they were associated with and leaders of the Irish-American societies in the states. He told them that he was the guest of the Duke of Devonshire at the castle, and that his sister was Lady Kathleen Hartington. They were aghast – it was outside their world – they could hardly take it all in.

"I really want to know if you can remember or know of any connection directly from the village with my family," he asked. They could not help him. "Have you any family who will take over the farm?" he asked.

"Oh yes," said Bill. "We have a family – two sons and a daughter – our eldest son lives in Australia and we don't know where our second son is since he left home. Our daughter is happily married and lives in Dublin, they have two lovely kids who like coming to the farm ever so much but they will never come to live here – there is no future for young people here and when we go this place will go just like all the others."

They wished him goodbye – they were delighted with his visit and insisted, much to his embarrassment, that he accepted their gift of eggs and butter.

The news of his visit spread through the village like wildfire. It was the main topic of conversation in the village shop and the pub for weeks.

"Did you have a good day?" said Kick as they met before dinner. "Find out anything interesting?"

"I had a great day," he said. "The couple I met were most helpful and interesting. I got quite a lot of background history but I was not able to pinpoint a direct lineage."

She laughed. "When you get home and tell Father he'll easily lap it up – he'll want you to tell this story to all the Irish-American crowd, he'll make as much capital as he can out of it – our true Irish antecedents!"

"You are quite right, Kit," said Jack. "Still this sort of thing is par for the course when you are on the political trail."

34

Kick, in the meantime, was recovering from her loss. The Devonshires, who were very fond of her, allowed her the use of their London house. After Bill's funeral Kick tried to contact Mary. She found that, after the memorial service held for Joe Junior at the Roman Catholic chapel of the RAF unit where he had been stationed, Mary had left the cottage and gone away, leaving no forwarding address. It seemed that, like Kick, she had to break with the past and start a new life.

Things were gradually returning to normal in London, and Kick was once more back amongst the refined circle of the upper crust that she had enjoyed so much when she was first in London, doing the round of the clubs, the shows, the races and all the social events enjoyed by members of the Establishment and the very wealthy. Her indomitable mother Rose came over to stay with her for a time, and they went off to enjoy Paris together.

Amongst the crowd in which she mixed she met an impoverished Earl, Lord Peter Fitzwilliam, and fell in love with him. He had been married at the age of 21 to Olive Plunkett, heiress to the famous Guinness fortune. The marriage was a disaster: Olive became an alcoholic. Peter was always the life and soul of the party in the clique in which Kick mixed. She was warned that he was not a very good catch, but she couldn't see his faults.

Joe and Rose. not knowing of the affair, were trying to persuade Kick to return to the States and live amongst the family. She joined them early in 1948 at their home in Palm Beach. Before she went, Peter had not been able to give her any firm promises of the state of his divorce. When they were alone and Kick broke the news to Joe and Rose they were horrified.

"Whatever do you think you are doing?" roared Joe. "How can you possibly think of going ahead with this? You say that he is an Earl – what do we know about him? I was originally against you marrying Bill Hartington but I had to admit that the Devonshires could not have treated you better, I came to respect and like them. I do not give a damn for titles but how do you think they would view this mad escapade? I absolutely forbid you to take it any further."

"You cannot tell me what and what not to do," replied Kick, nearly in tears. "I have a right to live my own life and seek my own happiness. I am not trying to get another title; I love Peter. Of course I really loved Bill but I cannot live in mourning all my life, I truly love Peter and I intend to marry him."

"If you do I shall disown you," said Joe. "This time I mean it," he declared.

"I don't care what you say, Father, it will not make any difference – I shall marry Peter and live in Britain; I shall not come back to live in the States.' She hurried from the room.

Rose had not said a word, she was devastated. She agreed with Joe, but that this should come between them, Kick of all the children, the one she had always felt the closest. Joe sat looking into space then picked up the phone and dialled a long distance number – "Is that you, Ben? Joe here."

"Why the devil are you phoning me at home at this time of the evening Joe – are you in trouble?" said Ben.

"No, I'm not in trouble," replied Joe. Ben Schwartz was Joe's lawyer – they went back a long way. He was the senior partner of a very large and successful firm of lawyers and over the years he had guided Joe through all the pitfalls and problems of the many business transactions – many of them slightly suspect – in which Joe was involved, becoming very rich in the meantime.

Joe and Ben were close friends – they had no illusions about each other.

"Ben, do you have any contacts in London – who could make some very private personal enquiries for me? It would have to be kept very confidential."

"Yes, the senior partner of a London firm is a friend of mine. I think he would know the best person to deal with that," said Ben. "What do you want done?"

"I want to know everything I can about a guy named Lord Peter Fitzwilliam. What's his financial position, what's his background, what's the state of his divorce proceedings? Any information about the guy you can get," said Joe.

"Sure, I guess they'll be able to get that for you, I'll lay it out tomorrow. Care to tell me what it's all about?"

"It's a very personal family matter, Ben, I'll tell you all about it when we get the report. Thanks a lot – appreciate it. Goodbye, Ben."

"Goodbye, Joe. Best wishes to Rose." Joe replaced the receiver and turned to Rose – she didn't say a word, she just nodded her head.

* * *

To keep Joe from feeling that he was being kept out in the cold, President Truman asked Joe to go to Paris to attend the international discussions which were to take place on the implications of the Marshall Plan.

Like Roosevelt, Truman was proving to be a very able President and, like FDR, did not want Joe to be too near the Administration in Washington – but he had to keep him sweet.

Before he left for Paris, Joe received a package from Ben Schwartz.

Dear Joe

I am enclosing the report I have received from London. You did not tell me when we discussed this what was involved but I have read the report and realise just how very concerned you are. Let me know if you wish me to take any further enquiries or any legal action. I hope that you will be able to persuade Kick not to go ahead with this marriage.

Yours
Ben.

Joe sat down to read the report – the more he read the more angry he became.

"Rose," he called, "Please come in immediately." As she appeared he pointed to a chair.

"This has come in from Ben," he said, 'it is the report from London about Peter Fitzwilliam. It is terrible – it appears that he has always been one of the crowd: the top flight, the best Club, the Races, everything to be in the swim, and apparently his reputation is not at all good, especially among the ladies. He met a young girl who fell head over heels in love with him – her name was Olive Plunkett – yes, Rose – the Irish Plunketts, the owners of Guinness – and Olive Plunkett is the heiress to their fortune. Despite all the families' efforts to persuade her otherwise she married him. They have now learned that he was quite impoverished – all the family assets were mortgaged and he had debts everywhere. They had to protect the family fortune and he had to accept a marriage settlement which he did not like but had to agree to – he was given a very generous annual allowance but if the marriage broke down and they parted he would lose any rights to his wife's assets and of course the annual allowance. As they predicted, the marriage was a disaster – he went gallivanting off as before, his wife took to drink and is now an alcoholic."

"Oh, Joe, this is terrible – whatever can we do?" said Rose.

"It gets worse, the family are now starting to take divorce proceedings against him, and, according to the report, have enough evidence to cite Kick as co-respondent in the proceedings."

"But that's not what Kick said," replied Rose. "She said that he was divorcing her, not the other way around."

"I think that this guy is a very smart operator," said Joe. "I suppose he thinks that after he is divorced and marries Kick, he will be well set up – she has a very generous income from her late husband, and he thinks I shall continue to make her an allowance."

"Whatever can we do?" Rose was quite distraught.

"I'll think about it," replied Joe.

Later that evening Rose sought out Joe and said, "Talking about that terrible news, Joe, I forgot to tell you that I had received a letter from Kick. I had written to tell her of the new appointment you had taken up in connection with the Marshall Plan and that you were going to Paris to attend the first international conference. She told me that she and Peter were going to spend a holiday in Cannes round about that time, and would it be possible for you to meet them one lunchtime? She said they could fly from London to Paris in the morning and then fly on to Cannes after lunch She said that she was so anxious for you to meet Peter."

"Yes, Rose, I can arrange to get away from the conference at lunchtime and I can meet them then. You'll find the dates in my diary, fix everything for me with her."

"You won't lose your temper will you, Joe?" replied Rose with some concern.

"No Rose, I shan't lose my temper – I'll listen to what they say, see what I think of this Peter and ask about the divorce. I'll say to Kick that when they have returned from their holiday we want her to come to the States so that we can discuss details – I'll show her the report then. I tell you, Rose, I'll move heaven and earth to stop this marriage taking place."

* * *

Kit jumped up and hugged her father as he joined them in the lounge of the hotel where they had agreed to meet.

"Pa," she said, "this is Peter."

"This is a great pleasure to meet you, Mr Kennedy. I have been looking forward to making your acquaintance. I have heard all about you and your work in Washington – a great pleasure indeed," gushed Peter. Joe sized him up:

tall, very good-looking, smartly dressed, club tie, obviously one of the upper crust – he could well appreciate that women would go for him.

"Yes, I wanted to meet you," said Joe. "When we heard of your friendship and plans to get married we were of course very concerned for Kick's future happiness."

"I can assure you that Kick and I are very much in love, and I will do everything I can to make her happy," he replied.

"Of course, before you can take this any further there is the question of your divorce. I presume that it is now being finalised and that your wife has accepted the position and that there is no reason why it should be delayed. I can have your assurance that Kick will not be in any way involved or mentioned, it would be very embarrassing to her and members of the family. As you no doubt know we have very close connections with the Irish-Americans in the States and I understand that your wife is a member of the Guinness family."

"You need have no qualms on that score, Mr Kennedy," said Peter. "I would not do anything likely to embarrass Kick or yourself, I love her so much."

"I am very pleased to hear that," said Joe. "Then of course there is the question of marriage settlement. I do make Kick a generous personal allowance. I presume you do not have any personal financial problems?"

"No, you can be sure that there will be no problem on that issue," Peter replied.

"I'm very pleased we have had this talk," said Joe. "I am glad that the divorce proceedings will soon be finalised. Kick – your mother and the family would like to hear all about your plans, and there will be quite a few loose ends to be tied up, so when you have returned from your holiday, I want you to come across home for a few days and we can formally discuss the details."

"Of course I will, Pa. I'll look forward to coming, and thank you for being so helpful and understanding."

"I am sorry that I have to leave, I've a conference meeting very shortly so I'll have to say goodbye." He kissed Kick and waved to Peter. "I hope you have a good holiday and a good trip – the weather looks shocking outside."

He left the lounge, entirely seething with anger. The two faced bastard – I'll see him in hell before this marriage takes place.

Before going in to the conference he phoned Rose. He gave her the gist of the conversation.

"Did you like him?" said Rose.

"Like him? I wouldn't trust him as far as I could throw him. He's smarmy and he grins too much. Still, Kick's agreed to come over – then we will have the showdown."

After Joe had left the lounge, Peter ordered two more drinks. "I told you that there was no need to worry, Kick. I thought that went off very well, your father seemed more than satisfied with everything. He seemed most friendly – he virtually agreed to our getting married. It's all going to work out fine." He was more than pleased with himself: the meeting had gone off far better than he had hoped for – he had expected Kennedy to ask far more awkward questions. Things did seem to be working out well.

Kick was not quite so sure. She knew her father's moods. Today he had been far too cooperative. She felt that behind his pleasant mood what he was saying was not what he was thinking, she had seen it all before – she hoped she was wrong.

They were sitting in the small lounge at the airport, waiting to board their small private plane – it was pouring with rain, no break in the clouds.

"I'm sorry, I am afraid we will not be able to take off, the weather is far too bad." The pilot had come to report the bad news.

"What do you mean, can't take off? Of course we can take off – do you think we are going to sit here all night, just because you don't want to take off because it's raining?"

"Don't you appreciate that the weather is so bad I do not think we should risk it?"

"Well, I do," demanded Peter "What do you want me to do, phone through to your London office that you are refusing to fly us on just because it's rainy? Are you going to fly us on, or shall I phone?"

The pilot bit his lip. He knew his company would not want to upset important customers – these clients were all of the moneyed class, and this so-and-so was just the type who would smear him and the company.

"Very well," he said "but I still do not think we should go."

Half an hour later they hurried across the tarmac in the blinding rain and boarded their plane which took off into the clouds.

They encountered a most violent storm. The small plane went out of control and crashed in a wood. The bodies of Kick, Peter, the pilot and his co-pilot were found in the wreckage.

Joe, in Paris, was told of the accident and hurried to the scene. He had the heartbreaking task of identifying Kick's body. He returned home to share his grief with the family. The Devonshires, as she was their son's widow, arranged for her to be buried with her husband in his grave at

Chatsworth. In deference to her religion, it was arranged that a High Mass be sung at a memorial service for her at the Roman Catholic church in Farm Street, London. In true Devonshire tradition, a special train took the body and a large number of mourners, including Lady Astor and Anthony Eden, to the committal at Chatsworth.

Kick's relationship with Peter Fitzwilliam had become known in the American Press and had been given a lot of not very complimentary publicity.

When the news of her death was reported, the *Boston Tribune* made it headline news: "Lady Hartington, next to the Queen, would have been the most powerful woman in England. Her tragic death ended the speculation that a Boston girl of Irish ancestry would have been in that position."

And so the unlikely connection between two powerful families with such different backgrounds – one which acquired great wealth in a short space of time in the jungle of modern business and financial juggling in America, and the other whose great wealth was acquired over centuries by inheritances and by inter-marrying with similar privileged personages – was ended.